# Remember the Red-Shouldered Hawk

# Remember the Red-Shouldered Hawk

DORIS BUCHANAN SMITH

G. P. Putnam's Sons · New York

*G. P. Putnam's Sons, a division of The Putnam & Grosset Group,*
*200 Madison Avenue, New York, NY 10016.*
*G. P. Putnam's Sons, Reg. U.S. Pat. & Tm. Off.*
*Published simultaneously in Canada. Printed in the United States of America.*
*Book designed by Gunta Alexander. Text set in Bembo.*

*Library of Congress Cataloging-in-Publication Data*
*Smith, Doris Buchanan.*
*Remember the red-shouldered hawk / Doris Buchanan Smith.*
*p. cm. Summary: Twelve-year-old John-too is dismayed when his grandmother,*
*who has come to live with his family, begins to experience increasing incidents*
*of confusion and memory loss. [1. Alzheimer's disease—Fiction.*
*2. Old age—Fiction. 3. Grandmothers—Fiction.] I. Title.*
*PZ7.S64474Rd 1994 [Fic]—dc20 93-14405 CIP AC*
*ISBN 0-399-22443-2*
*10 9 8 7 6 5 4 3 2 1*
*First Impression*

*With love to my brother,*
*Jim Buchanan,*
*who shared the strange last days of our mother,*
*Flora Edna Robinson Buchanan*

# Remember
# the Red-Shouldered
# Hawk

# Chapter One

On March 19 I began disappearing from my grandmother's mind.

Mom and Dad had gone to the mountains to move Nanna, to bring her to live with us here. I had looked out the door, walked into the yard and even to the middle of the street forty-two times. Looking. The forty-third time, as though my presence had finally summoned them, here they came. Nanna's face was beaming from the windshield of Mom's car, and Dad followed in the U-Haul truck.

Like a happy idiot, I shouted and jumped and waved. The ruckus brought all the others to the porch. By the time Mom pulled into the driveway the entire family was in the yard shouting and waving. Even Louis was joining the enthusiasm. He had just learned how to wave.

As soon as the car stopped I yanked open the door saying, "Nanna, Nanna, Nanna."

"Well, give me just a minute," she said, gripping her purse and twisting in the seat and sliding out. I didn't want to give her a minute. I wanted to hug Nanna now.

Everyone was crowding, but I kept my position for first hug. With that marvelous Nanna smile, she glanced around at everyone and then, as I knew she would, focused on me. I had grown. For the first time, my arms reached all the way around her. The tips of my middle fingers touched and she felt as sturdy and solid as ever. She patted me on the back and shoulders and didn't ruffle my hair.

"Well, whose boy are you?" she said, and everyone laughed.

"I'm your boy, Nanna." I squeezed her again. Though everyone in the family loved her, there was no doubt in anyone's mind that I was her boy.

She took me by the shoulders and maneuvered me back a little to make room for the other hands and arms reaching for hugs. When my twin sisters were born more than twenty years before me, Nanna had been working full-time and traveling a lot and she didn't have the chance to spend a lot of time with them. My nephew Adam, who was my age and my friend, was born in Puerto Rico and lived there until five years ago when he was seven, so she hadn't really attached to him when he was little, and I had a head start on him with Nanna. Nanna's face was smothered with kisses, and my other nephew, Louis, who had just learned how, gave her a sweet kiss. Nanna took one of his bare feet in her hand and gave it an affectionate shake.

"And who is this little one?" she said. "It must be Iris."

We all laughed again because Louis was a replica of Iris.

Rubbing her fingers across Louis's toes, Nanna looked over and beyond the people to the yard. "Ahhh, wisteria," she said, taking in a deep breath and naming every blooming thing. "Redbud, dogwood, pear, azalea, forsythia, quince, pansies, daffodils, sweet William. So many colors."

Ahhhh, I thought. Nanna was here. And Nanna was Nanna. She was okay.

"That's what I like about the South, having all this in March." Dad pulled off his sweater and squeezed into the crowd and put an arm around Nanna. We all knew what he would say next, and he did. "If I could just bottle this air . . ."

Nanna grinned. ". . . you could sell it and make a fortune."

They said this to each other like a comedy routine, but they alternated roles. He said it here on the coast of Georgia and she said it in the mountains of north Georgia.

"I think what Mother Vee needs is a tall glass of iced tea. We've had a long ride." Mom draped one arm around Nanna's shoulder and with the other made motions as if she were shooing peacocks. She meant us. I nodded. Dad had called to say it was a slow trip, teasing me, saying that Nanna was doing my act. "I have to go to the bathroom. I'm hungry. Can we stop and get something to drink? How much longer until we get there?"

I had laughed, of course, because it did sound like the way I used to be up until a couple years ago. But it didn't sound like Nanna. She always enjoyed the trip as much as the getting there. She called herself a traveling fool. I guess we were all traveling fools. Mom and Dad were folksingers and traveled all over the world, and sometimes I went with them.

We parted ranks and lined the sidewalk as Nanna and Mom walked up toward the porch. We eyed one another in anticipation as they approached the ramp my brothers-in-law had built. On any trip anywhere, in spite of having to hobble because of an arthritic knee, Nanna refused to give in to a ramp. At the bottom of the stairs she paused, looking at the ramp and those five steps. She sighed as though they were as high and steep as Mount Everest, but set a foot on the stairs. Then she turned toward the ramp, put a hand on the railing, and walked slowly up.

*"Viva!"* Edgardo shouted, prompting a chorus of applause and cheers. Spanish sprinkled our conversation because we were all fluent. Dad and Mom had learned it in college and taught Iris and Rosie long before Rosie met Edgardo in Puerto Rico. But never a word of Czech from Nanna. She'd left it behind when she left the home country when Dad was a boy.

No sooner was Nanna clear of the sidewalk than Dad was backing the truck up the broad sidewalk and we scrambled for the stairs.

"Excepting babies and women over forty, all able-bodied persons are hereby invited to the great unloading." That only left out Nanna and Mom, and I followed them across the porch and heard Nanna's question as we neared the door.

"Where is this? What place is this?"

"This is our house in Hanover, Mother Vee." Mom spoke softly and quickly, as though expecting such a question.

"Well, yes, I know that. But what place is this? Whose house?"

I made a quick intake of breath and held it while Mom answered smoothly. "This is our house, your son John Viravek's house. Now your house, because you wanted to come live with us and we wanted you to come."

The truck was at the porch, and letting down the gangway seemed to propel me through the door. Behind was the safety of doing some physical task. I had a necessity to be with Nanna. Mom poured iced tea only for the two of them and gave me the shooing motions.

"I want to be with Nanna." I was trying to get over being stunned. I knew the reason she was here, and that knowledge, which I'd tried to ignore, whizzed through my head while Mom waved her hand at me.

A month ago, Nanna had gone for a ride and gotten lost. For five days. There had been a three-state alert for her by the time she was found. There had been no foul play. She had just been lost. A battery of tests showed she was in good shape physically: good heart, good blood pressure, good everything else they knew how to check. But she was disoriented, confused.

It was as though someone had made up this story, because Nanna was the least confused person I knew. It was impossible to believe "the traveling fool" had been lost for five days.

"Nanna's here now. There will be plenty of time."

Miserable, I retreated toward the hall door.

Behind me Nanna said, "Who is that boy?"

The question didn't startle me. Nanna was only teasing me again. But Mom's answer speared me in the back.

"He's my boy, Mother Vee," she said as though it was a serious question. "He's your boy. Your grandson John-too."

With my mouth hanging open, I glanced back. Mom shooed me one more time.

"I am not a peacock," I shouted, and I sort of rolled around the door frame, plastered my back to the wall, and sank to the floor. All the things reeling through me were scary to think about. The incident of the Cheerios rose up and threatened to smother me. Last summer when I was visiting her, Nanna had bought four boxes of Cheerios at the store when we had just bought four boxes the day before. I reminded her we already had four boxes. Checking the new batch through, she said, "Well, you can never have too many Cheerios."

I had repeated this to the family as a funny story. But my parents hadn't thought it was funny. They began to watchdog Nanna and I was sorry I ever told them.

"Heads up, John-too. Here comes a parade." I looked up to see the entire family bearing down on me. My sisters marched toward me with bedside table and lamp. According to my parents' instructions, we had earlier cleared and cleaned the front bedroom for Nanna's things. Behind Iris and Rosie were Adam, and also our neighbor Broderick, struggling with Nanna's orange velvet chair. I didn't even know Brod had come over, although he'd stopped by several times while we were waiting for Nanna. Seeing him brightened me a bit. My brothers-in-law were about to run over them all with the bed. Dad, standing near the living room door, was the Louis cuddler of the moment. He started singing work songs to the baby, "Yo ho heave, ho," and everyone immediately joined in. When the parade moved into the bedroom, I reached for the baby. If I couldn't have Nanna, I at least wanted Louis.

"Sweetheart, we have a million boxes to unload."

"A trillion!" Broderick said.

I looked through the living room and across the porch into the back of the truck. "A quadrillion," I confirmed glumly. I wished I'd gone to my room.

14

I glanced into the kitchen expecting Nanna to have turned into a white-haired old lady with a face like melting putty, but she looked the same. No one who didn't know it thought she was anywhere near eighty. She had almost no wrinkles and Dad teased her about her fourteen gray hairs.

I scurried through the kitchen, giving her a quick, sneak-attack kiss on the way and saying, "I love you, Nanna. I'm glad you're here."

"I might be glad, too," Nanna said, "if I knew where it is I am."

I whizzed on out, trying to outrace the attack from Nanna's remark. Did she really and truly not know where she was?

The enormous stack of boxes wiped unwelcome thoughts right out of my head. "What are we going to do with all these?"

"For now," Dad said, "why don't we make a box fortress along the front wall in the dining room. Stack them along the floor and up between and beside the windows."

"Yeah, a fortress," Brod said, hefting the first box, and the box parade began.

I was glad Broderick was here. He had been my best friend since we were three. He had no grandmother of his own and had adopted Nanna.

"Try to stack them so we can see the labels," Dad said, carrying a box and directing us to group certain types of things together. "Can you believe these were the leftovers after we'd eliminated a lot of stuff? This part is easy compared to the packing."

The labels read sheets, towels, bathroom things, kitchen things, paperweights, bells, demitasse cups, hand-painted china, ceramics, egg art. And more. Much more. Dad called Nanna the whatnot queen of the world. The china, ceramics, and egg art were things she had made herself. In all there were thirty-five boxes. That wasn't a zillion, but it did make quite a stronghold stacked along the dining room wall.

"What's wrong with Nanna?" Broderick whispered as we brought in the last of the boxes. I glared at him for saying it out loud, as though saying it would make it so. I glanced toward the kitchen door, but I don't think his whisper carried that far.

I set my box down with a sigh. Label out. Bathroom things. "It's just the confusion of the move," I said. "You know how, when you've been skating a long time and take the skates off, they still feel like they're on? Like that."

Rosie and Iris called for an inspection of the room. So now we had another bedroom parade, all of us in there before they brought Nanna, as though she would inspect us as well as the room. The bed was made, the Oriental rug was on the floor. Everything matched. Nanna was a matching sort of person. Nanna was impressed.

"How did my things get here? They look lovely, don't you think?" As she admired the room, she moved around, stroking things. We all agreed. I had Louis again, and I jiggled him a bit while we had one more parade to settle down in the living room.

Nanna's eye traveled through the wide doorway into the dining room.

"What's all that?"

"Your boxes," Adam said.

"It looks like I'm moving in."

"I think you are. I think you have." Dad perched on the edge of the sofa back and rubbed her shoulder.

"I have my work cut out for me, then, don't I?"

I laughed and relaxed. Nanna was Nanna. And she was all right.

"Here." I noticed she still had her purse on her arm. "Let me take your pocketbook to your room."

"No, no," she said, gripping it firmly as I reached. "I'll just keep it with me."

I nodded. Obviously, she didn't feel at home yet. Well, she would. Her own sofa and whatnot shelf unit had also been put in the dining room. She would have family and some of her own things around her.

For a closer inspection of her boxes, she stood up and walked into the dining room. Then she patted the arm of her sofa and disappeared into the kitchen and I followed the sound of her footsteps. Through the kitchen and into the hall to the bedroom, then back to the hall and kitchen, to the hall and down it toward my room, then back up to the kitchen and bedroom.

When she reappeared she said, "Come see my room."

Rosie laughed, but she got up immediately, and so did Mom and Iris. Then Nanna came for Dad, Patrick and Edgardo. Adam, Broderick, and I muffled our amusement. We heard Edgardo say, *"Maravilloso."*

Next she corralled the three of us boys. "Come see my room." We came. We saw.

Then she started over again and repeated the procedure.

"I think I'd better be getting home," Brod said. At least he could leave. He didn't live here. Adam didn't, either, but he lived too far to walk so he had to wait until his parents were ready.

"Let's go to your room," Adam said. "I have something to show you."

I hunched a shoulder. Part of me was anxious for the solitude of my room, but the other part didn't want to leave Nanna. Only if I stayed with her would she settle in and know that this was now her home. When she began yet another round of repeats, Adam stifled a giggle and poked me in the ribs. I poked back, hard, to let him know it wasn't funny. Last summer Cheerios were funny, but I'd learned too much in the past hour or so. I had lost my sense of humor where Nanna was concerned.

As Rosie started off to see the room one more time, Adam grabbed her hand and held her back. "Mama, why does she keep wanting to show us her room?"

As Adam whispered to his mother, we heard Nanna ask, "Do you like the way I've fixed it?"

This question was new, anyway, and I heard the others laugh at Nanna's joke.

Rosie whispered back to Adam. "Just pretend you're an actor in a play and you have to go through the same situations day after day, saying and responding to the same lines while making it seem like it is new and happening for the first time."

After everyone had admired the room enough times, Nanna was finally satisfied that we'd all seen it, and we settled back in the living room again. But she continued strolling around the house looking, interested, curious, with her purse dangling from her arm as though she might be leaving any minute. After several minutes she stuck her head into the living room.

"Can someone tell me where there's a bathroom? There doesn't seem to be one on this floor."

I looked at Mom, at Rosie, at Iris in alarm. She'd visited this house and used this bathroom for years, and she had just walked past the open bathroom door several times. There was no other floor.

Rosie recovered first, matched Nanna's polite tone. "It's pretty simple, Nanna. You just keep walking around until you find a toilet."

I gasped and Adam jammed my ribs again, but Nanna continued her walk and soon called out with the pleasure of great discovery, "I found it."

When she was inside with the door closed, everyone but me doubled over in muffled laughter. Even baby Louis laughed in response to the laughter.

"How can you think it's funny?" I asked in an angry whisper.

"How can you not think it's funny, John-too?" Adam said, ready to poke me again.

*"Uncle* John-too to you," I said, cocking my elbow for an unaccustomed jab at him, but he was too quick for me. I stood with my elbow sticking out like a bird wing, scowling at them all.

"I'll Uncle John-too you," he said with a pretended jab.

"It's black humor," Dad said when he'd regained his breath.

"What does that have to do with anything?" I looked at Edgardo, who was coffee-colored. No cream. My question made them all laugh again.

Patrick saw my puzzlement and winked. "It's not humor about the color black or about or by black people. It's reverse humor. Like when something painful or sad or unhappy happens but there is something funny in it anyway. Gloomy humor."

"Like having heavy clouds hovering inside your head but something *cómico* happens, anyway." Edgardo pronounced "hover" to rhyme with "over" and waggled fingers above his head to demonstrate "hovering."

"And it's okay to laugh," Patrick said, patting my back.

I still didn't see anything funny.

"That's what helps us survive," added Rosie.

"We shouldn't have brought her here," I whispered. "It's too much for her, the mess of packing, the moving, the long drive. All these people. We should have left her alone."

Dad curled me into a hug. "Oh, my sweetheart. My dear sweet son. We probably left her alone longer than we should have. This was already happening. We just hadn't noticed what a hard time she was having."

Until the Cheerios story last summer. They noticed when I told the Cheerios story.

"Uncle Jim says it seems to be happening pretty fast," Mom said. Uncle Jim was Dad's brother, who lived an hour away from Nanna in the mountains.

I wanted to close my ears, shut myself away from all of them. I should have accepted Adam's request for us to go to my room. At least I would have missed this part. The laughter was over. We all looked up as Nanna returned from the bathroom.

Almost immediately she lifted an empty arm and said in alarm, "My purse. Where is my purse?"

"You must have left it in the bathroom, Nanna," Iris said.

Nanna looked as though Iris must be an idiot. "In the bathroom? Why, no. Why would I take my pocketbook to the bathroom unless I'm at a restaurant or something?" But she turned around, anyway, stepped back into the bathroom, and returned with it in her hand.

"I'm getting to be such a forgetful old lady. But I'm eighty years old. What does it matter?" Laughing at herself, she swung the pocketbook toward us and back, beckoning us one and all. "Come see my room."

# *Chapter Two*

When I woke up to get ready for school, Nanna was still sleeping. I stood at her bedroom door, waiting a minute before I had the nerve to twist the knob, crack the door, and peek in. We had a standard policy in our house not to disturb sleeping people unless you knew they needed to be awake for something. But I had to be sure she was all right.

At the sound of the door she opened one sleepy eye and peered at me. I waved and blew her a kiss.

Just then Mom snagged me, arm curled around my waist, and pulled me back.

"I saw the red-shouldered hawk," Nanna said, blowing a kiss and waving back as the door clicked shut.

Mom tugged me across the hall and into the kitchen. "Honey, you're the one who said we should have left her alone. We couldn't leave her alone in the mountains, but let's leave her alone here as much as we can. You know how she loves to sleep late."

"But she remembers the red-shouldered hawk," I whispered. I spread my wings and soared around the kitchen.

I wondered if Nanna'd dreamed of one. But she remembered the hawk and that meant she remembered me.

On a pass by the cereal cabinet I grabbed the box I wanted with my talons and landed lightly at the table. "Where's Dad?" Though we often had do-it-yourself breakfasts, we usually ate together when everyone was home.

"Still sleeping, too. He's exhausted from our days of packing and moving."

I nodded. I understood. But I wanted him here. I wanted everyone here, for this rejoicing. The hard part was over. Everything was going to be all right. All Nanna had needed was a good night's sleep.

The cereal whispered into my bowl and crunched in my mouth. I was grinning all over myself, happy again about Nanna. She had taught me to love birds and watch for them, telling me what to look for quickly, before they flew away. Shape, relative size, thickness of beak, wing and eye markings. Hawks were pretty easy to identify as hawks. The hard part was deciding which kind of hawk it was.

On the way from here to my sisters' once, Nanna and I had seen a red-shouldered hawk and stopped to watch it. The broad, banded tail was distinctive, she said. This stretch of marsh beyond the River Bridge was apparently its territory, because we saw it there many times afterward. But only that first time had we seen it suddenly drop from sky to earth and come up with some small catch. Maybe a marsh mouse. And Nanna remembered.

I put my bowl and spoon in the dishwasher, returned the cereal to the cabinet, and kissed Mom good-bye. As I went through the dining room, the box fortress filled my eyes. I'd help her unpack the boxes, unless she wanted to do it herself, which was the way she usually did things. In her own way and her own time. She had lived alone all these years since Dad and Uncle Jim left home.

Out the door and there was Broderick, waiting in front of his house on the next corner. So we were back to our old routines. While Mom and Dad were gone I'd stayed out at the game farm with my sisters and taken the school bus with Adam.

"How much further did you get on your computer game?" was Brod's first question. "Did you figure out how to make the leaves drift?"

I was still drifting with the hawk, but I dove down and caught reality. "I was out there and my computer was here, so how much do you think I got done? Zip." Brod and I were computer buffs, the only two at school who had learned to program anything besides what we called "baby games."

"My biggest problem is typos!"

"Yeah," I said, but I was still with Nanna and the joy of hawks. "Do you remember me telling you about the time Nanna and I saw a hawk catch a mouse?"

"It would help if we'd learn to type," he said.

"Adam has been trying ever since to see it for himself and get a picture of it."

Adam was a hunter, with a camera instead of a gun. He lived in the woods and stalked trees, plants, and animals and had some amazing pictures. Even some night pictures of owls. My brother-in-law, his Uncle Patrick, had all sorts of photographic equipment and loaned Adam such things as telephoto lenses and nightscopes.

"I figured by now you'd have those leaves drifting," Broderick said. I could see we were having two sets of dialogue. As we climbed up and through Lover's Oak, I concluded I could enter his conversation more easily than he could enter mine. Climbing through this immense tree was a ritual of ours, like it would be bad luck not to do it. I jumped from the north side of the tree, and Brod, behind me, landed like a feather. He was more agile than people thought for being stocky. Brod was a brick.

"Before I have the leaves drifting like I want, I have a lot of lines to write." My game was currently called Falling Leaves, with computer people trying to catch the leaves in a basket or rake them off-screen.

"I have Galactic Warriors almost done," he said, chattering on about his game. "Maybe we can get together this afternoon to proofread each other's programs."

I hunched and shrugged, both nodding and shaking my head before I said, "Yeah, maybe." I didn't know what I could do this afternoon until I saw how Nanna was doing.

"Well, the science fair is in six weeks."

"Good grief, Brod. That's not quite tomorrow. We could do forty-two programs by then."

"Not forty-two. It's taken us weeks to get this far."

"So, I exaggerated."

We had already started our projects before we even knew the date of the science fair. Now we were working on a mutual project with computer games. Computer talk carried us nearly to the school gate, where Brod made a U-turn back into my conversation.

"It will be fun to have Nanna here, won't it?"

I looked at him, wondering why he hadn't picked up on this subject at the beginning. "Yeah. It will." I guess maybe he had been trying to ignore Nanna's unusual behavior, too.

As we walked through the gate, Adam's bus pulled into the unloading circle. Broderick and I met the bus as it rolled to a stop. "Yo," Adam said, hailing us as always as he hopped down from the bus. "Look what I've got." Moving up beside him as he opened one of his books, we saw he had some photographs.

"What're those?" Brod asked, leaning close to see the one on top. I couldn't figure it out myself. It was like some Druids romping around in the woods, sorcerers in high, pointed white hats, or something.

"Hey, Adam, what ya got there?" a schoolmate called out, and stepped toward us. Adam snapped the book shut.

Only after the book was closed and I saw the photo in my mind's eye did I know what it was. I was about as familiar with the Ku Klux Klan as I was with Druids. "Where did you get that!" The startled sound of my voice attracted attention from some of the others crossing the school yard, and in a moment we were surrounded. They clamored to see, and when Adam wouldn't show, one of the boys snatched the book. Quick as a cricket, Broderick grabbed it back and hugged it to his chest with his arms crossed over it.

"If you want this book, you have to go through me first." Immediately the reaching stopped and the crowd dropped back to beside and behind us. Broderick was tough as well as sturdy. A bulldozer. Nobody messed with Brod.

"Adam has girlie pictures," someone yelled. The cry went up and out and we were nearly mobbed. I almost laughed.

Adam was so squeaky-clean. He would never have girlie pictures. But I was puzzled as to why he had the pictures he did have. But I knew no one else had seen them but me and Broderick.

Even while being mobbed, Adam talked about it as we moved toward the building. "You should have been there. I was sneaking around trying to get a shot of a nighthawk."

"A nighthawk?"

"He just has a picture of a bird."

Near the building and in the proximity of teachers, the disappointed crowd drifted off in various directions. Brod slid the book back into Adam's stack.

"You want me to keep it for you?"

"Nah. Who's going to try to snatch a picture of a nighthawk?"

"Yeah, well." Brod stopped at Mr. Hamlin's door, and Adam and I went on to Ms. Johnson's.

"Why in the world did you bring them to school?" I whispered, unheard by anyone but Adam in the hurly-burly of the hall.

"I had them yesterday. That's why I wanted to go to your room, but we were busy with Nanna and there were too many adults around," Adam said as we walked into the room and over to our desks.

I sat down thankful for that bit of judgment, anyway. Just what we needed, to throw pictures of the Ku Klux Klan into the mix with Nanna. She'd want to know where they were and go after them with her moral indignation.

The final bell rang and Ms. Johnson began taking the roll. My head snapped left to Annajoy. Boy, was I distracted.

The first thing I'd done every morning for months was look at Annajoy Soo. She gave me joy. And pain. The pain was my own problem, from not being able to let her know I liked her. And now there was more pain because Brod had started noticing her and talking about her, and to her. Some boys seemed to talk to girls like they automatically knew how, but I wasn't one of them. How did you learn? I asked my parents about so many things, but I didn't seem to be able to ask them about this.

"John-too? John-too?" It was Adam whispering and poking me with a finger. Ms. Johnson had called my name.

"Present."

"Well, you woke up," Ms. Johnson said. My classmates, and even Ms. Johnson, laughed at me because she was finished with attendance. Viravek was the last name.

I shifted and stuck my feet out into the aisle and tried to keep my eyes off of Annajoy. The sight of her creamy skin and her straight black hair made me lovesick. I looked anyway and wondered what trouble this would make between me and Broderick. He had expressed his liking for her out loud and I had kept my mouth shut. He'd never believe I liked her first, and what difference would that make, anyway? The difference would be if she liked one of us. My advantage over him was that she was in my homeroom and two of my classes and only in one of his. At least I could start the day off looking at her.

In addition to being my homeroom teacher, Ms. Shelley Johnson was also my history teacher and she was almost as pretty as Annajoy, but her hair wasn't as dark or as straight. During history, I couldn't concentrate, but it wasn't only because Annajoy Soo was three desks away. I kept seeing Adam's picture. Did he mean the KKK had had a meeting right behind his house? And Nanna kept wandering around in my head, lost. I wanted to run home to see about her, but I reminded myself she remembered the hawk.

In science class Mr. Hamlin outlined some possibilities for science projects, "because you need to be thinking about it." He excused me and Brod to go to the computer lab, since we were already working on our project. We spent the time whispering about Annajoy. Rather, Broderick whispered and I thought my own Annajoy thoughts while I listened. Other than that, the day dragged by, and when the afternoon bell rang, I was so anxious to be with Nanna that I ran off from Brod and Adam, intending to run all the way home.

Since I had last class with Adam, I shouted a "See ya" to him and fled. Brod saw me and ran with me.

"Hey, what's the hurry?"

"I'm just wanting to be with Nanna now that she's rested a bit."

"Did Adam show anyone else those pictures?" he asked.

"I don't think so."

"He shouldn't have brought them to school."

I shrugged.

"He shouldn't have taken those pictures. That's private business."

"I guess so." I shrugged again. "It's scary business."

"Oh, I don't think it even happens anymore."

"Then how did Adam take a picture of it if it didn't happen?"

He shrugged and I shrugged again and said, "Let's run."

We trotted toward the gate, and just outside, with no provocation I knew of, Brod reached out and grabbed one of our classmates by the collar and yanked him back and down. Then he fell on him and started a fight. I grabbed his collar and pulled.

"Broderick, stop it. What are you doing?" My tugging at his collar was like a flea trying to drag the dog. But a couple of others joined in, one tugging and the other shouting in his ear. "Okay, Broderick. We know you're tough. Come on, get off of Molo."

In the brief pause Molo slid out from under Brod. I was so stunned I didn't say anything. Molo was very tall and several of his friends were there and I was certain there would be a terrible fight. He merely brushed himself off, with his friends helping and patting his back, and headed off opposite the way we would walk. Brod shook his head and snorted like a stallion and turned toward home.

"What in the world got into you?" He had always been feisty, quick to take offense if he thought someone looked at him cross-eyed. Something must have happened between them during school because as far as I could see, Molo was just minding his own business.

"Doesn't anything bother you?" Brod's tone was absolutely hateful.

"Are you angry with me?"

"You are always so reasonable."

The sidewalk was made of hexagons and I did some footwork to step in every segment. "There are worse things."

"Don't people like Molo bother you?"

I looked back as if I thought I could still see Molo, which I couldn't, as if to examine him to notice what I'd missed.

"That's what I mean. You don't get it. People like that. People who have stupid names like Molo. Can you imagine being named Molo?"

"I kind of like it. It's different. I like unusual names."

"Sure, *John.*"

"Viravek," I countered. "And it's Jovan in Czechoslovakia."

"There is no Czechoslovakia."

"So hooray for you, you're up on your central European history."

"So I guess you can speak Czech, too."

"Are you angry because I can speak Spanish?" Nothing was getting cleared up for me. I was only more confused.

"You can be so dense sometimes, Jo-van. I mean *certain* people with stupid names. Certain dark-skinned people."

"Oh, come off it, Brod. Do you even hear yourself? You mean dark, like Adam? Do you mean unusual names like Adam Festivo?"

Broderick tilted his head one way, then another, as we continued down the hexagon sidewalk. "Yeah." The head movement turned into a nod. "Maybe that's exactly what I mean. Adam's even darker than Molo."

"And his father is even darker than Adam. You're right, Broderick. You know central European history and you're observant. And I don't get it. Adam is your friend."

We were at Lover's Oak. Brod climbed up and through and I just stepped over the roots. I didn't even want to be in the same tree with him. Except for Annajoy's, I'd never paid that much attention to skin. In our family my two brothers-in-law were the lightest and the darkest. Patrick was blond, freckled, and his father was Irish. Edgardo was a dark Puerto

Rican. We'd been to Puerto Rico at least once a year while Rosie was living there and they had all shades of people, just like the United States, though no freckles. His hair was as dark as Annajoy's, and she was Korean. Adam took his color from his father.

Feather-foot Brod plunked heavily when he jumped from the south side of the tree. "Well, maybe he's not my friend if he brings pictures like that to school."

"Hey, I don't think it was too smart for him to bring them to school, either, but why does it upset you so much?"

"If he'd been caught," Brod said. "If *we'd* been caught when we were all looking at it . . ."

I shrugged and raised my free hand. It didn't sound like much of a problem to me.

At the corner by his house his father was in the yard, raking live-oak leaves, which, strangely, fell in the spring and not in the fall. When he saw us he leaned on the rake.

"Well, news travels as fast as the crow flies," he said. "I've already heard you've been in a fight."

Not that he'd care, I thought. He'd probably be proud.

"Yes, sir," Brod acknowledged. "A nigger started something with me."

"Bro-od." I jumped—at the word and the lie.

Mr. Shaw raked a few more strokes. "I trust you finished it."

With a fierce kick into the pile of leaves that disturbed them hardly at all, Broderick said, "Yes, sir. I did."

Without another word between us, he stomped off toward his house and I stepped off for mine, feeling Mr. Shaw's power behind me. The memory of an early incident with him was still clear. Brod and I had been friends since we were toddlers and even then he was always hitting me. I didn't like it but I didn't ever hit him back or stop being friends. One day his father told me to hit Brod back. He mistook my refusal for fear and held Brod's hands behind his back, both small wrists in one large father-hand. We were about five.

"Hit him back," Mr. Shaw commanded. "I've got hold of him. He won't hurt you. Don't be a sissy. Hit him back." At my reluctance, he continued urging me. "Just ball up your fist and hit him." He demonstrated how to make a good, tight fist.

My hands refused to curl into a fist, and quite on their own, they crept behind my back.

I looked up at him and said, "I don't like to hurt people."

# Chapter Three

Our house was one story, but large, with a high roof flanked and hovered over by two of the enormous live oaks. There were also dogwoods and pines, and from the angle I approached, it looked like it was built in a forest and not in a neighborhood of small yards. Because of this and my inattention, I didn't see Nanna on the porch until I was going up the stairs.

"You look mighty glum for a boy on a sunny day," Nanna said. "Do you live here?"

I couldn't even get a grin on my face and take her remark as teasing. "Yes. I live here." I plunked into the low lawn chair near her.

"I've been sitting here bird-watching. The birds have been flying from here to over there and from over there to here." Her hand and arm flew back and forth, indicating the path of birds. Even as we looked, mockingbirds perched on the power lines, cardinals searched the shrubbery for berries, and blue jays squawked from everywhere.

"Do you remember the red-shouldered hawk?" I asked.

"Oh, the red-shouldered hawk. Yes." Her face was bright

and happy and it was almost Nanna back. "Once I watched one drop from the sky and catch a vole."

I laughed. The hawk had caught something too small for us to see from the distance, so it hadn't been a rabbit. But a vole? How like Nanna to name something specific.

"Yes, I was with you when you saw it. We saw it together."

She looked at me, smiling, not a trace of confusion on her face or in her eyes. "Oh, I remember that hawk, but I don't remember that anyone was with me."

I scraped my chair close to her and put my head right in her lap as though I were Louis. Her purse was in her lap and I set it on the floor. "I was with you, Nanna." Then I almost wailed, "Nanna-a-a, I want you to remember *me.*"

She raised herself slightly, as if to shake me from her lap. I shook. I sat up and scooted my chair back.

"I apologize for not remembering you, but I haven't had time to get to know everyone yet. I just moved here last week. And what is this Nanna business?"

I gulped air and dragged my chair forward again. I reached out and took one of her hands and looked at her eye-to-eye, my brown ones to her blue ones. "You are Nanna," I said. "You are my grandmother, Valerie Viravek, and I am your grandson, John-too Viravek."

"Oh, I'm getting to be such a forgetful old woman. But I'm eighty years old. What does it matter?"

I rubbed her hand. "It matters to me, Nanna."

The door opened and there was Dad. "I thought I heard talking out here. Look, Mother. John-too. Isn't that an orchard oriole?"

I looked, and it was, right in the dogwood tree nearest us.

*35*

A small black-backed bird with orange underneath. I remember calling it the Halloween bird when I first learned it, and I wondered if they were here all the time or just passing through from south to north. Except for in the mountains with Nanna, I'd never seen one.

"Oh, I don't know their names," Nanna said. "I just enjoy them."

Dad pursed his lips in a sort of "Oh, okay" expression, but it wasn't okay with me. I howled.

"Nanna, you taught me the orchard oriole."

Smiling, thoroughly enjoying the bird, she said, "I don't think I've ever known the name of that bird."

For some reason this struck me worse than her not knowing me. For twelve of her eighty years she had known me, but she'd known the birds forever. She was the one who had taught me about orchard orioles and hawks. I stared at the fading gray boards of the porch floor and wondered if stomping on them would pound her memories back into her. I wanted to insist and argue her memory back.

"Watch it for me while I get my camera," I said to both of them, and I ran to get it.

I returned to the porch quietly, whispering, "Is it still here?"

"Right there." Nanna pointed.

It was so tiny I was sure it would just be a dot in the picture. If Adam was here, he could use Patrick's telescopic lens. I wasn't a photographer, just a point-and-click snapshot taker. As if wanting its picture taken, too, a mockingbird landed on the railing just the other side of Nanna.

"Well, I'll be . . ." she said softly.

Turning just a bit, I got an excellent shot of Nanna with the mockingbird on the railing beyond.

Without a word to either of us Nanna pushed herself up and hobbled past Dad and into the house.

"Enough of birds, eh?" Dad said as she passed.

"Oh, well, no. I always enjoy them, but I want you to come see my room."

Now, that *was* funny. I didn't understand my moods, how it could have been so unfunny yesterday and so funny today. If Adam were here, I'd poke him in the ribs. So Dad and I took another room tour.

"How do you like the way I've fixed it up?"

"Mother, we brought your things here and fixed up your room for you. Don't you remember all the packing?"

There was a wince in his words and I looked at him quickly. What a clunkhead I was, I thought, so busy with my own feelings, I hadn't even considered his. This was his mother. We were all disappearing from her mind.

"I have to do my homework," I announced abruptly, and fled to Mom. But as slowly as Nanna walked, she was right behind me, coming to the kitchen. I rolled my eyes and grimaced to Mom and took off to my room. I wanted to be three and have someone to hold me while I cried and cried and cried. Instead I flung myself belly-down on my bed, face in pillow, and lay still except for my lower legs. One at a time I lifted them and pounded them onto the mattress the way I wanted to pound the floorboards of the porch. *Thwack, thwack, thwack.* What's the matter with Nanna? *Thwack . . . thwack.* It's just the move. When I was little I sometimes did this to alleviate frustration, pounding things out of myself. I never knew why, but it had been so satisfying. It still was.

Eventually I stirred and moved over to my computer, which brought Broderick to mind. I wasn't going to thwack the computer, but I was wondering, What's the matter with Brod? Brod wasn't confused by a move. How could he act so strangely, in a way I had never seen before? Not the attempted fight, but the words about Molo and Adam.

I turned on my computer to avoid the "whoops" that rolled through my head. I had never heard Brod use such a word and I'd never heard his father use it, either. But I suspected the word came from Mr. Shaw. Maybe Brod was changing, maybe he was getting more like his father.

The flickering screen and the electronic dit-dit-dits of loading the program pulled me quickly into the computer world. Soon I was lost in working on my own game.

Some people say computers are "smart," but I knew that some person or persons had to be smart first. A computer wasn't really "smart," but just tedious when you were trying to program it and tell it what to do. And marvelous fun for those who liked it. I did. So did Broderick. I raked him out of my head the same way my little computer characters were raking leaves off the side of the screen. I already had that part done, choice of a boy or a girl or both catching leaves in a basket or raking them off the screen. The leaves that weren't caught or raked piled up across the screen so that if the raker's head was covered with a pile of leaves, the game was over.

I hated the violent games. Shoot, smash, bam, boom. I was determined to make some games that were gentle, but still exciting and fun. Titles was the hard part. A game called

Falling Leaves didn't sound very exciting. I was still thinking about titles.

Drawing the boy and girl and programming their moves was hard, but the drift of the leaves was even harder. I had to program every tiny incremental movement down or left or right or the fraction of a rotation. The concentration of doing this kept Nanna out of my head, but Brod kept drifting in, like the leaves. Brod, Brod, Brod, Brod. A couple years ago someone had asked me how I could be friends with someone like Brod. I didn't know. I hadn't thought about it before or, much, since. We were just friends, that's all. I didn't have to be old and gray to know that no one is perfect. Not even friends. Not even me or Brod.

Now I felt sorry about running off from Nanna and left to find her. Not that she would even notice or mind, but I did. She was back on the porch.

"Nanna, why don't you come see the game I've made for my computer?"

"Oh, I don't know a thing about computers." She waved her hand the way she'd waved it to indicate the flight and directions of birds. She had enjoyed learning a few things about the computer before. I got a sudden burst of wisdom and did not try to tell her that.

"It's just typing. You've done that a lot. Come on."

"Oh, my typing days are over," she said. "I don't think I can even do it anymore."

But I kept trying until finally she came with me. She exclaimed over the color on the screen as though she had never seen it before.

"This is a game called Falling Leaves," I told her. "See the leaves I've made? Sugar maple, red oak, and yellow poplar?''

"Oh, I don't know the names of them," she said. I put a finger against my lips and pressed hard. I'd never seen a tree she didn't know the name of. She knew more trees than birds because, she had said, birds wouldn't stand still while you checked them out.

I had drawn the trees in five sizes, each in its proper autumn plumage. At least she admired the leaves, even if she could no longer name them. I tried to show her the arrow keys so she could direct the basket. I didn't even try to show her how to choose either the basket or the rake. She couldn't "see" the arrow keys. Since a typewriter didn't have arrow keys, she was blind to them. She enjoyed watching me for a while, enjoyed the color and motion of the leaves. Then she said, "You come to my room. Come see my room."

I did, then returned to my computer and got lost in it. Creating autumn in Hanover was a treat, because Hanover in reality was semitropical. Autumn in Hanover didn't shout itself to the world, it whispered. And not until late in November. You had to look close.

I was working close, so totally involved in fine-tuning the drift of my cloud of leaves that the click of the door opening startled me into a jump.

"Sorry to disturb you in your sanctum sanctorum," Dad said quietly, "but it's our turn to fix supper. Reality must be served."

I shook my head, not to say no, but just to shake myself into transformation from computer whiz to kitchen boy.

"It's okay," I said. And it was. At least my parents understood this out-of-the-world concentration. They not only sang folk songs but wrote them, too, and privacy in their studio was maintained. Dad called the studio their sanctum sanctorum, which meant private place. There was no such place as that in Brod's house. At least not for Brod. No matter what he was doing, his parents just yelled for him—to come, to go, to wake up in the morning, to go to bed at night.

I gathered my reality-serving wits to leave my room.

Dad sat down on my bed. "Can we talk a minute?"

"Sure." I sat in my desk chair.

"I don't mean to intrude, but I happened to be checking on Nanna when you and Brod came around the corner. I saw Mr. Shaw having an exchange with Brod, then Brod sort of stomped into his house and you walked away with a very determined step. Do you have a problem with Mr. Shaw?"

I looked around my room as though I had never seen that stuff before. The light green walls. The spread with Pac-Man figures all over it. My dresser with my old Tootsietoy collection on top.

"You can see all that looking out a window?"

"Well, yes. I guess so."

I ran my tongue around my lips and told him about Brod jumping Molo and what he'd said about Molo but not what he'd said about Adam. "By the time we got home Mr. Shaw had already heard about it and he was quite proud of Broderick. Brod was stomping away from me. I didn't like what he did and said about Molo and I said so. And he didn't like my saying it. Sure, he gets in fights sometimes, and sometimes he picks them, but I've never heard him talk like that before."

Now Dad examined the Pac-Man bedspread, running a

finger in circles around first one figure, then another. "What are you going to do about it?"

I hunched a shoulder. I hadn't even let myself think about it. "Nothing, I guess. Just avoid him."

"Well, I'm not going to tell you what to do," he said. "You have good judgment. But you might think about the fact that prejudice is a learned behavior, which means that it could be unlearned. And who better than you to try to help Broderick unlearn it?"

I just hunched the other shoulder. I wasn't even ready to consider such a thing. I just wanted to take care of myself and let Brod take care of Brod. If I had to stay out of his way, then okay, fine.

Dad clapped his hands and stood up. "Mom suggests we try to involve Nanna with supper. She is so disoriented. She isn't sure where she is or who we are."

I moved on out of the room and toward the kitchen. I didn't want to hear anyone say these things out loud.

"Of course, she was that way at her house, too," he said behind me.

I slung open the refrigerator door and attacked.

By the time Dad said, "Hey, whoa there, we're about to have dinner," I already had juice, fruit, and cheese in my hand.

"I'm starved. I didn't have my snack. Dinner will be at least a half hour, won't it?" I took a bite of apple, a bite of cheese, and washed them down with a swig of orange juice. It was true I hadn't had my snack, but mostly I wanted the action of biting and chewing to erase the thoughts that were buzzing around in my head like stinging bees. I heard Nanna mumbling in the dining room and stepped around the corner.

"Unpacking?"

"Oh, no. I'm not unpacking. I'm just sitting here wondering who all these boxes belong to and when they're going to get them out of here." She waved her arm as if she were a magician and could make them disappear.

In the kitchen Dad set squash and onions and a knife on the cutting board. "Will you make squash casserole for us?" Dad winked at me as he spoke to Nanna. "You always made the best squash casserole. Good enough for me to like it as a boy when most children wouldn't eat it."

Nanna raised her back, shoulders, and head until she was three inches taller. "Well, I used to make a very good squash casserole. I don't know if I even remember how to do it anymore. And I don't know why I should be expected to when there is a paid staff here to do it."

"Oh, no, Mother. No, no, no, no. There's no paid staff here. Just us. You, me, Claudia, and John-too. And you don't have to do anything you don't want, of course, but nobody makes squash casserole like you do."

Nanna looked bewildered. "Do you have all the ingredients?"

Nanna had probably made a thousand squash casseroles in her life. And the squash and onions were on the counter. Where had my Nanna gone?

"Sure," I said, forcing a grin to my face. "And I'll help. I'm an expert bread crumber."

Dad took chicken and the makings for a salad out of the refrigerator and handed me the sack of old bread.

"Would you rather cut the squash while I chop the onions? Or would you rather chop the onions while I cut the squash?" I held up the squash and onion.

Standing facing the room with her arms slightly raised, she looked suspended there, ready to speak or move but not speaking or moving. Dad and I just waited. Finally she said, "I'll cut the onions. Do you have a scuba mask?"

Now Dad and I stood speechless, motionless. Then I blinked, and again I thought clearly and acted quickly.

"Sure," I said, "I'll get it." And I did. I had no idea what world this was or what world she was in, but I brought everything, mask, fins, and breathing tube.

"Goodness. I don't need all that." Nanna reached out and took only the scuba mask.

"What's this for?" she asked about the breathing tube. I told her. "Well, I don't think I need that, and what do you call these flipper things?"

"Flippers," I said. "Or fins."

"I don't need them, either, but they should be fun, don't you think?"

Sure, Nanna, I thought. I snorkel across the kitchen every day at suppertime. It's a regular habit of mine.

She took the fins, too, sat at the table, took off her shoes, and slid her small feet into the fins.

Dad busied himself skinning and deboning chicken, trying to act as though his old mother in scuba fins was the most ordinary thing to have in a kitchen. I wished Adam had been here to see this. I'd give him a poke in the ribs.

"Well, I think I'm about ready," Nanna said. She flipper-flopped to the counter, tucked the scuba mask under her nose, and pulled the strap to the back of her head as if she did it every day. The rubber of the mask pulled a tuck in her upper lip the way it did mine. Or anyone else, I guess. Picking up an onion, she peeled it, sliced it, and started chopping.

Dad and I managed to look at each other without cracking up. He shrugged and I shrugged and we busied ourselves with our own chores.

As the knife snip-snipped against the cutting board, Nanna said, "This is the best way I know to keep the onions from making me cry."

# Chapter Four

I had run to my room for my camera and snapped pictures of Nanna in the fins and scuba mask. And now, Saturday, we'd taken the film to be developed and had lunch and wandered around the mall while we waited for the pictures. Nanna did a lot of sitting on benches. She had totally lost her power walk.

As we strolled toward the exit I ripped into the package of photos and rifled through them looking for Nanna in the scuba mask. I stopped in my tracks. There was Annajoy Soo looking out at me over Adam's shoulder. Annajoy in my hand. My camera had not been used for a while and I had forgotten taking these pictures at school, maneuvering a bit so I could catch Annajoy in the background.

"They must be good, the way you're smiling," Dad said.

Quickly, I shuffled through the stack until I found the pictures of Nanna. "They are great," I said, stopping them in the parking lot to look. "Ohhhhh, look." Nanna was delighted over the orchard oriole, then exclaimed at herself and the mockingbird. "I've never had a picture of myself with a bird." When she saw herself in the Cyclops lens of the scuba mask, she heehawed. A good old Nanna laugh. "But what are those things on my feet?"

"My swim fins."

"Well, I know they say the camera never lies, but this camera lied. I've never had anything like that on my feet in my life."

"How about a scuba mask?" I asked. "Have you ever had one of them on?"

"Well, of course. I always wear one of those when I'm chopping onions. I must have been chopping onions."

Mom, Dad, and I joined the hilarity, but none of us had ever seen Nanna in a scuba mask or ever seen one at her house. We had discussed it thoroughly the night of the squash casserole, which, when she sat at the table and began to eat, she didn't remember making. As we were getting in the car Nanna stopped and stood staring into space. Or, as it turned out, at Mom.

"And do you always wear that hat?" Not only had Mom had it on her head since we left the house, she'd had it on her head for years.

"Always." Mom grinned. "John bought it for me the first time we sang in Guatemala." It was a rather floppy straw hat with a purple, red, orange, and lime-green band, the fringed ends of which fell toward the edge of the brim. That hat was older than I was.

"I don't like it," Nanna announced.

Mom laughed. "Well, Mother Vee, I'll remember not to ever ask you to wear it."

In the car I, too, laughed, but only to myself. I had seldom heard Nanna be critical and had never heard her be rude. It surprised me to realize that there were things I didn't know about someone I knew so well. Like Nanna and scuba masks. The way she and Brod were acting.

The pictures in my hand reminded me there were things Brod didn't know about me. Annajoy, Annajoy, Annajoy! I felt myself grinning at the picture of Annajoy while puzzling over what Brod and I had not shared. Brod was in some of these pictures, too, of course. Even Molo.

It had been a rough week. Brod wouldn't talk about why he jumped Molo or why he lied to his father, and Adam wouldn't talk about the KKK picture, and I hadn't made any progress with Annajoy.

"Does anyone need to stop back by the house for anything before we head on out to the bird zoo?"

Dad's voice brought me out of my private meanderings. I had scarcely realized we were rolling along and I was here in the backseat with Nanna. I touched Nanna's hand. "Nanna loves the bird zoo."

"I don't know what it is," she said, "but it's all right with me."

"You know. The game farm. You're the one who always calls it the bird zoo."

"Aren't the others coming?"

"That's where the others live, Nanna. They don't live with us, they live at the bird zoo."

When we rode, Nanna usually gave a running commentary about the sky, the trees, the birds, the flowers, the water, but she was quiet today. The day was all green and blue, trees and sky, and the twelve-mile ride out to the game farm was always fun. Town was left behind quickly as we headed for the River Bridge, which crossed Hanover Harbor and connected the mainland to a stretch of marsh. The harbor spread east around Golden Isle to the Atlantic Ocean. The center span had to lift for freighters, but the shrimp trawlers could always get under, even at high tide. Neither were in sight at the moment. Gulls floated on the air currents, and sunlight winked across the water. The marsh grass was turning from gold to green.

"Now watch for the red-shouldered hawk," I said as we descended the bridge. "Remember, it sometimes perches on top of the telephone poles." This stretch of marsh before we came into woods again was its hunting territory.

"Yes," Nanna said. "Once we saw one dive for a vole just as we happened by. Look, there it is now, on top of that pole." We all ahhed our confirmation, and as we watched, it spread wings, dropped from the pole, caught a current, and drifted above the landscape. I was soaring myself. Nanna remembered the hawk and she'd said "we." I hugged the memory to myself and turned in my seat to watch the hawk for as long as I could see.

We were rolling along the straight, flat south Georgia road toward other birds—quail, grouse, ducks, pheasant, turkey, geese, and all manner of feathered fliers bound for someone's table.

When Rosie and Edgardo had moved back from Puerto Rico to start the game farm with Iris and Patrick, we had all pitched in; even Nanna had come down for a month. We had been everything from carpenters and carpenters' helpers to lumber, wire, nail, and water carriers. We hammered together buildings for a hatchery, a feed shed, a shipping center and office, but the most amazing construction was the flight pens.

None of us but Edgardo and Rosie had ever heard of a flight pen before, much less seen one, or helped build one. High, wide, and long, the pens were fenced across the top and were large enough for the game birds to fly and keep healthy.

When the birds arrived, Nanna and I had been appalled to learn why the birds were being raised. I don't know what we thought. Surely they wouldn't have that many birds just for pets. They were to be sold to restaurants, grocery stores, and hunting preserves.

"Have we not had chicken dinner at your house?" Edgardo had asked in response to Nanna's expression of horror. Back then his English still had an equal measure of Spanish accent and his words came out "cheeken deener." And "theenk" when he said, "Where you think they come from?"

"But these aren't chickens," she said.

"Well." He picked up a quail. "Thees is just a leetle cheeken." He set down the quail and scooped up a pheasant and stroked its head. "And thees is just a beeg cheeken."

It had seemed a bit traitorous to eat a bird you'd been friendly with. But my conscience had been eased by many good meals. Besides, Patrick said only vegetarians had the right to protest.

After marsh and woods and more marsh and woods we turned left through a pine forest that opened onto the game farm. The house was low and long, a duplex with a common room at the center. As soon as the car stopped, I leaped out and opened the car door for Nanna.

"No, no." She waved away my extended hand. "I can manage. I've been taking care of myself for eighty years."

Outside was only grass and gravel, and since anything other than paved, level surfaces was difficult for her, I took her arm. I was afraid of her falling. She shook off my arm and immediately nearly tripped over the hose coiled by the spigot near the steps.

"Watch out for the hose!" I grabbed her arm again to tug her away and nearly pulled her over.

Pow! She gave my arm a fiery slap. "People don't realize that when they hold onto me, they pull me right off balance." Nanna's voice stung like her smack, so I was stung twice.

At the three shallow steps to the front door I made my arm as firm as possible and held it out to her, for her to hold me instead of me holding her.

"That's the way," she said, putting her hand on my arm. "Thank you." I could feel the difference in her step now that she had control of her balance. She was steadier and hobbled less.

"Well, you're here." The doorway was filled with Rosie, and Iris holding Louis, and we were all busy with hugging. I saw Nanna go stiff. My sisters had been on the phone with Mom, but they hadn't seen what I'd seen all week, Nanna being so uncomfortable with everything and everyone. As we walked in, Nanna focused her attention on the baby and I knew she did not know who these people were.

"These are the others," I said, trying to help her with a clue.

"Well, I know that," she said.

Something clutched me inside to watch her try to fake her way along. Acting interested and curious, she looked around. For the past several years this had been one of her favorite places. Whenever she came to our house, the first thing she wanted to do was come out to the bird zoo. I waited for her recognition.

From this center room the house stretched out east and west, into a full house for each family, the Festivo side and the Kelly side. Everyone thought this a perfect way for twins to have a house. Totally separate, but still together.

I saw Nanna's eyes cross the room to the window that overlooked the yard and the game pens beyond. We followed her across.

"What are those? They look like indoor tennis courts. But they're outdoors."

"Yes." Iris laughed. "That's what you said when we built them." The flight pens could easily accommodate several games of tennis.

"Those are the flight pens," I said.

"What do they fly?"

"B-b-b-b-b-*buh*," said Louis as though he knew exactly what we were talking about and was trying to say "Birds."

"Birds," I said to Nanna and to Louis. "This is the bird zoo."

"Oh, I've been to zoos hundreds of times and all of them had birds. But I've never been to a zoo that had only birds."

"Mother, you've been here a hundred times, too," Dad said. "This is the game farm. You remember that Rosie and Edgardo and Iris and Patrick started the game farm. You even helped. Remember?"

Nanna crossed her arms over her chest and stood taller. "It's rather irritating for people to keep insisting I remember things that I don't remember, and the reason I don't remember is that I never did them." She rubbed her arms and I watched her struggle to figure out how to fit herself in with these people. These strangers. Us.

"What kinds of birds?"

"Let's go see." I opened the door.

"Adam, Edgardo, and Patrick are out in the incubation shed," Iris said, hoisting Louis to her hip.

As soon as we were out the door, Louis stretched his hands out clutching for the birds. He was only eight months old, this second nephew of mine, but he knew what was out there a hundred yards away.

We walked slowly with Nanna, who was holding Dad's arm. Her purse, which had been lost daily during the week, was gripped in her free hand.

I reached out for Louis, and Iris handed him over. The tender feel of him always made me melt. Since Mom and Dad had been pretty old when I was born, Louis was as close to a baby brother as I'd ever have.

Beside us a peacock strutted and Louis leaned out, reaching for it. As if in pleasure of being noticed, the peacock fanned his tail. This, and Louis's reaching out, popped an idea into my head. Adam had given peacock feathers to everyone who wanted them, but I never had. I looked around for a molted one and picked it up. For Annajoy. She probably had one, but this one would be from me.

Nanna exclaimed over everything. "I've never seen anything like it," she said one moment and, "Oh, I've seen this a hundred times," the next. I thought my eyes would roll right out of my head.

Dad winked at me.

"We have some quail hatching, Nanna," Iris said. It was one of her favorite things.

Dad and I headed for the incubation shed with Nanna while Mom, Rosie, and Iris went back to the house with Louis. Adam's red all-terrain vehicle was parked outside by the shed.

The minute we stepped inside we heard the "Mexican jumping bean" rattle of the eggs.

"Would you look at that," Nanna said. "Are they really going to hatch?"

"Hey, John-too!" Adam called. We did our routine of greeting with our hand-slapping and bumping arms and hips. He tilted his head toward the door.

I shrugged and watched Patrick and Edgardo show Nanna the eggs that were already cracked. I looked at Nanna, feeling bound to her, unable to move away from her, even though I wanted to go with Adam.

"Come on, let's go," Adam said, his voice stomping on the "go." My head wobbled back and forth and I was unable to choose.

Dad winked at me again. "Go on."

Edgardo picked it up. "Shoo, shoo, shoo. No *niños* allowed today."

As soon as we were outside I was ready to hiss in Adam's ear, "What about the picture?" But he jumped on the ATV and started it and the roar was so loud all I could do was hop on behind and hold him around the waist. He veered past the flight pens and scattered peacocks as he drove along the trail beside the marsh. He didn't drive too fast, but not too slow, either. At the place where the alligator sunned in summer he stopped.

"The alligator's back, see?" There was a mud slick where the gator slid into the marsh creek from the bank and it had been recently used.

"How big is it this year?"

"Haven't seen it yet."

Last year it was about four feet long and we saw it regularly. It disappeared during the winter, holing up somewhere in a burrow beneath the creek.

Before I could ask him about the KKK picture he was back on the vehicle and we were bounding through the woods. He stopped to show me deer spoor and he shhhed me as we left the vehicle and walked to a tree where there was a sleeping owl.

"The barred owl I told you about," he said as he motioned me down. On our bellies with chins in hands, he whispered to me about the Ku Klux Klan meeting across the narrow inlet of inland marsh. He had been out with Patrick's night-scope trying to photograph a nighthawk.

"Broderick was pretty upset that you'd brought that picture to school."

"Hmmph," Adam said. "I didn't think he was afraid of anything."

"He was afraid that if you got in trouble, we would, too. For looking at it."

"Why would I get in trouble? Tell him there is a law about freedom of information." He picked at leaves and pine straw before he said, "We've had threats."

"Adam!"

"Not because I took pictures. Before that. In fact, we didn't know they were meeting over there. Maybe they're not. Maybe that was just one time. I hope."

I lowered my forehead to the ground cover of leaves, soft

from wintering over. "I hope, too," I said across my arm. I was frightened to even be looking. Then, ashamed of my ostrich behavior, I looked up again and seemed to see them weaving whitely among the trees.

"What kind of threats?"

Adam stared out at the marsh for a long time, as though searching for the alligator, or maybe an otter.

"They called Dad a nigger."

Our silence was immense.

"But he's not," I said.

More silence, then an explosion by Adam. "Does that mean you think they only made a mistake, that it's okay to make threats to other people?"

"No, no."

"Don't tell Grandma and Grandpa. Promise. Dad and Uncle Patrick don't want to upset the family."

"Well, Rosie and Iris know, don't they?"

Adam shook his head, and his hand and arm shook beneath his chin. "We don't think anything will happen, but Mama and Aunt Iris would worry."

More silence while all this wobbled inside my head until, for some reason, I had a need to fill it. "We saw the red-shouldered hawk on the way out."

"Same place?"

"Yeah."

"Catch anything?"

"Naw. Flying, though."

"I'd like to get a shot of that sometime."

After pushing to his feet, he led me slowly and quietly back up the path.

"Want to drive?"

"Of course," I said, and he climbed on behind me.

Back aboard, I jounced us over the trail of small hills they'd made in this flatland. This might be an all-terrain vehicle, but flat was all the terrain there was in southeast Georgia unless someone unflattened it. I weaved figure eights and various other geometric patterns among the pines, gunning it a bit on the straightaway. The vibrations stirred and shook and dissolved Adam's revelations.

"Go to the mailbox," he yelled in my ear.

So I headed toward the house, past it, and down the driveway to where the mailbox perched near the highway. I maneuvered close enough so Adam could reach without getting off. He opened the mailbox and shoved the pile of mail into a canvas tote bag that hung like a saddlebag. Back at the house everyone was drinking iced tea or soft drinks and eating cookies and cheese crackers. Adam and I didn't even pretend to be mannerly, we just chugalugged the tea and took two handfuls of cookies. Amid the crunch of cookies, I heard something chirping. "What's that?"

"Nanna's baby quail," Iris said.

My eye followed her eye and there in a box beside Nanna was a newly hatched quail.

"Nanna's?" Adam and I said in chorus. My mind was wiped clear of other thoughts.

"You know how Patrick and Edgardo always try to tease her into taking one for a pet?"

"Nanna, you've never had a pet," I said.

"Maybe not," she said, "but I have one now. Look." She put her hand into the box, against the bottom, and by the time she had it there, the Ping-Pong-ball-sized quail had hopped into her hand.

I was dumbfounded. Nanna didn't like pets, had never wanted one, never allowed Dad to have one, and he, in turn, had never let me have one.

"You're supposed to say, 'Awwwww,' " Rosie said.

Suddenly Nanna raised her hand and looked to either side of her and to the floor. I knew what the problem was before she said it.

"Someone has taken my purse."

Everyone immediately looked around.

"She had it when we went out," I said. I remembered noticing it clutched in her hand. "I'll go get it." In one week I had become the expert purse finder. I ran out and Adam with me. We hopped on the ATV and zoomed to the hatchery shed, trying to hold on while still stuffing cookies into our mouths, popping in one after the other.

"This happens all the time," I told him. "We call them the lost-purse episodes." Sure enough, there was her navy-blue purse on the floor of the hatchery shed. She must have put it down when she was concentrating on the quail.

I picked it up and we started back. At the house with the motor shut off Adam said, "She forgets things a lot, doesn't she?"

Mouth full of cookies, I nodded. When I had swallowed, I said, "Yes, but at least she doesn't show us her room anymore."

# Chapter Five

The quail was named Janek, and I got some wonderful pictures of Nanna with it in the palm of her hand. And since she had a pet, I thought it would be mine, too, but she kept Janek shut up in her room and kept me shut out.

We were surprised at her giving it a Czechoslovakian name because she had put Czechoslovakia behind her when they came over. She had given Dad and Uncle Jim American names and started calling herself Valerie or Val instead of Valeska, and worked hard to lose her accent. She didn't speak Czech, and Dad and Uncle Jim didn't either. The name John in Czech was Jovan. So if she hadn't changed Dad's name, I might be Jovan-too.

The whatnot queen of the world had opened two boxes but not unpacked them. In the dining room squeezed in beside the box fortress, her whatnot shelf still stood empty. When we offered to help, she said, "I'll do it, I'll get around to it." But she didn't, and some days she didn't even realize they were her boxes. The boxes upset her on the days she thought they were all hers and on the days she didn't.

I thought going to the game farm would have helped her to remember things, especially who "the others" were. But she had some "others" we couldn't fathom. At mealtimes she still asked, "Aren't the others eating?" or when we went out somewhere, "Aren't the others coming?" I rummaged through my snapshot box and made a collage with our pictures. Hers, mine, Mom's and Dad's, and Janek. On my computer I made colorful labels for the pictures and for the title, "Four People and One Quail Live Here." I surrounded the labels with flowers, trees, and one bird, to represent the mockingbird.

She read it solemnly, reached out, and rubbed my cheek. "Yes. Thank you for this. I think it will help."

I hugged her and she accepted the hug and I wished I'd thought of making something like this sooner. But I had never imagined she would have trouble knowing *us*.

At supper one night, Nanna waved her hand toward the dining room. "When is someone going to take care of those boxes?" We'd been eating in the kitchen because she didn't want to eat in the room with the boxes.

Mom, Dad, and I looked at one another, the frustration showing in their eyes and maybe mine, too. Then Dad brightened.

"After dinner." He nodded to me. "We're going to take care of that first thing after dinner."

And after dinner, we did.

"Four of them are yours," Dad said to Nanna, looking at the labels and choosing boxes of things he thought she might want or need soon. We carried those into Nanna's room and stacked them nearly out of sight in the corner between the dresser and the far wall. Then we started the second box parade as we trudged upstairs to the attic and down, upstairs and down, repeating the trips the way Nanna always repeated her questions or remarks. Dad made up a song about it.

> We're moving boxes to the attic,
> We will never more be static,
> We're moving the boxes today,
> Moving them out of our way.

As we carted boxes upstairs to the attic, Mother caught on to his song and joined in from the kitchen. Dad and I were breathless by the time we got done with thirty-one boxes. Now there was a box fortress in the previously almost-empty attic.

"I don't know why I was so slow to see that she can't deal with them," Dad whispered as he sat on his father's old army trunk. "She doesn't even realize they are hers." Sighing, he sank. Elbows to knees, chin to hands. "If she asks about something, we'll come find it for her, okay?"

"Okay." I stared at the trunk wondering if Grandpa Viravek, who was killed at the end of World War II and whom I had never known, knew what was happening to Nanna now. So many memories locked away inside that trunk, and inside Nanna, too. She never spoke about it, and when Dad occasionally did, I guess I didn't listen very well.

"We left her alone too long," Dad was saying now. "She's worse off than I ever thought." His lip quivered and tears tracked down his cheeks. Mine, too.

We heard the telephone in the distance and left it for Mom.

Dad looked up, ready to go down if Mom called him, but she didn't.

"I don't understand it," I said. "Why doesn't she know us? What's happening?"

"We tried to tell you, John-too. It's Alzheimer's disease. Or probably Alzheimer's," Dad said. "They can't really know for sure unless they do an autopsy of the brain after a person dies. It makes people forget things and sometimes even changes their personalities. Sometimes it progresses slowly, but Jim said this has been moving pretty fast with Nanna."

A shock went through me. It took extra breath to ask the question. "Is Nanna going to die?"

"Oh, well, we all die," Dad said, reaching out and grabbing me into a tight hug, nestling his chin into my collarbone.

The idea of Nanna dying was sad and scary. Even scarier was to think my parents could die, ever, much less while I was still a boy, which is what had happened to Dad.

Mom and Dad both said, "Death is a part of life." I understood the truth of it. I just didn't want it to happen to anybody in my life. I wanted them to live forever.

"The image of her in that scuba mask," Dad said. His head was out of his hand and he was smiling. "At least her sense of humor hasn't changed."

I slumped into the position he had just abandoned, chin in hands. "It might change mine," I said.

"Hot up here, even in March," he said, standing up and starting for the stairs. Hot or not, I didn't want to leave. Somehow I felt that if I sat here long enough with Dad, I could figure a few things out. Including what Adam had told me. A hundred times I'd almost told Dad, or Mom, but caught myself in my promise not to tell the family. Now

Dad's back was toward me and he was treading down the stairs.

"Oh, honey," Dad was saying as I came into the kitchen. "I didn't mean to leave you with the dishes." We had a household rule that the cook doesn't clean up.

"Oh, sweetheart, that's okay." They reached out for one another and danced around the room. "I'll exchange boxes for dishes any day."

"Oh, really? Next time I want to get out of the dishes I'll just bring the boxes down again."

Nanna was sitting in the dining room, on her sofa, and Mom and Dad danced that way, then put the whatnot shelf between the two front windows. Mom spread one arm and said, "Here, the shelves are ready for some of your things. The boxes are in your room. Shall we get one?"

"I don't think so. Not right now."

On the wall hung a pewter knife, fork, and spoon, about three feet high, obviously made for Paul Bunyan. Dad lifted down the knife, held it like a sword, and tapped the sofa, the table, and the shelves and Nanna's head. "I hereby dub this the Valerie Viravek Room."

Now Mom and Dad had danced around the dining room, each extending an arm to Nanna.

"The Valeska Room," Nanna said, holding out her hands. "Oh, my, how I used to love to dance. Oh, how Jovan and I used to dance." Mom and Dad each took a hand and I held out my hands and entered the group.

"Ta da, ta da, ta ha," Dad sang as we circled. As if also joining in with us, the doorbell rang its own "ta da."

"That will be Broderick," Mom said, releasing my hand and turning me under her arm and whirling me right out of the circle. "He called and wanted you to come over and I said why didn't he come over instead. So here he is."

I glanced at Dad, who quickly said, "I'll get it," and swung himself out of the circle. Nanna and I took hands and continued slowly while I listened to Dad greet Brod.

Then there he stood acting just like normal. We did have a détente in our cold war and had walked to and from school together all last week, but it wasn't normal. I had told Adam about Broderick and Molo, but the same as I told Dad, leaving out what Brod had said about him. All week I had not asked Brod to come over and he hadn't come or asked me to his house, either. And here he was, in my sanctum sanctorum.

First thing, he grinned at Nanna and spoke to her. It startled me to realize she had been like his Nanna, too. I clamped my teeth and felt my jaws knot up. I didn't want to share her with him anymore. Still, we were acting normal and we kept on acting normal.

"Nanna, you remember Broderick," I said, to remind her.

"Do you live here, too?" Nanna asked.

Brod hunched a shoulder and lowered one eyebrow, puzzled. "Well, sometimes it seems like it, I guess." Now, that was not normal because he hadn't been over for two weeks, not since the day she came.

"Well," Nanna said. "A lot of people live here. I thought maybe you were one of the regulars."

He looked totally confused.

"Brod lives just down the street," I said. "Remember?"

"No. Why should I remember? Am I a living address book? I don't keep track of where everyone lives."

I winked at Brod, gave Nanna a hug, and excused us to go work on our computers. As we left the room I heard Nanna asking, "Why does that boy keep hugging me? It's sweet, but . . ." We moved out of earshot.

"What's going on?" Brod was wide-eyed.

Before I could answer, the faint peeping of quail filtered through Nanna's closed door.

"What's that?"

I called back to the dining room. "Nanna, would you like to show Brod your baby quail?"

"Of course," Nanna said.

"A quail?" Brod said, because he knew as well as I did that Nanna didn't like pets. As kind as she usually was, when he'd brought his dog over to show her once, she told him quite bluntly to take it away.

Nanna came, opened the door, let us in, and closed it behind us saying, "What does my little Janek want?"

Brod made a surprised face at me and I nudged him toward the box so he could see.

Nanna leaned over, put her hand into the box, and Janek hopped into her palm. Broderick was properly impressed, then astounded when she set the tiny bird on the floor. He looked at me and raised his eyebrows. I nodded solemnly. Then she set a paper on the floor.

"Its name is Janek," she told him. "It's used to papers in the box so when I take it out, it will use the papers if it has to . . . you know."

"Edgardo told us that," I told Brod. "He had pet chickens when he was a boy and they were paper trained."

Brod's eyebrows headed for his hairline. "Where did you get it?" he asked, although I thought surely he should know. In this family, where else would we get a quail?

"At a pet shop," Nanna said. "I just walked in to look at

the animals and there was this little quail chick just hatching. I watched it hatch."

I let my mouth drop open. One of the few things she would never do with me was walk through a pet shop to see the animals. But good for her. She had part of it right, anyway. She did see it hatch.

"Oh, okay," Brod said, but he cocked one eyebrow at me.

Once again I excused myself and Brod, and we slipped out the door, being careful Janek didn't escape.

"*¿Qué pasa?*" he asked. He'd picked up a few Spanish words from us and liked to toss them into his conversation every once in a while.

"All the packing and moving and unpacking has confused her."

"I can tell," he said, the perplexed look still on his face. "She wanted to come here and live with you, didn't she?" In my room he drew up a second chair to my computer.

"Well, yes, but we don't always want what we think we want, do we? Remember last year when I thought I wanted to spend a month at computer camp and then I didn't like it all that much?"

"Yeah, well." We mused over it for about three seconds before he took his computer disk out of his pocket.

"I found out about Adam's picture," I whispered to him, and he stopped with his hand in the air. "The KKK had a rally in the woods across that little stretch of marsh behind their place." I continued whispering as though I might be heard in this back room with the door closed. "He was out with his camera trying to catch a nighthawk when he saw them."

"I don't even like talking about it," he said.

"Yeah. Scary, isn't it?" It was almost amusing to think of Brod the Hulk being afraid of anything. I remembered my promise to Adam, but Brod wasn't family, and Adam had shown the pictures to Brod himself and I hadn't told Brod about the threats. It was tempting, though. It heightened the power of secret. We were acting normal and it seemed normal, just like always having Brod in my room, us sitting in front of the computer.

"He asked me not to tell anyone," I said, trying to add power to my secret.

"Don't worry about that. I won't."

He popped his disk in and turned on the machine.

"I just don't understand all this hate." I was sitting in the chair beside Brod, but it seemed as though we were down on our bellies in last year's leaves, like Adam and I had been. Comfortable, compatible, sharing. I was thinking of the hate in regards to the KKK, but that reminded me of Nanna telling of her experiences in Czechoslovakia during World War II. In case Brod took my "hate" remark personally, like an accusation, I covered myself by babbling on.

"I mean there is such hate all over the world. All the wars. One group hating another and each one thinking they're right and the other's wrong so they don't listen to or respect each other's feelings or opinions." That stopped me because I was struggling to stay friends with Brod, but from whatever angle I examined it, I couldn't respect some of his opinions, like physically trouncing someone for any reason at all, much less for no reason. Hit, punch, kick, shoot, kill. Like his computer game, which he was already playing.

"What I *really* don't understand is that so much of it is

religious. The Protestants, Catholics, Christians, Jews, Muslims, and on and on and on." He was rat-a-tat-tat-tatting through Galactic Warriors, gunning down enemy spaceships and I couldn't resist one more category. "Whites, blacks."

He put the game on pause and looked at me. "I just don't think we should be talking about it."

I started to say something else, but stopped myself and reached over, unpaused the game, and started playing it myself. Rat-a-tat-tat, kill, kill, kill. How did anyone solve anything if they didn't talk about it?

"Hey, no fair." He imposed his fingers over mine and stopped me, which I knew he would, so it saved me from too much symbolical killing.

Warfare of various types seemed to be the favorite in computer and video games. I had thought about this war business a lot. I hated it. I had a poster that said, "War is not healthy for children and other living creatures." I agreed. If there was such a thing as a draft when I was old enough, I knew I'd be a conscientious objector.

Even though I didn't like the content of Broderick's game, I was impressed with the way he'd programmed it. We had each proofread and reviewed the other's program and game, so I had played Galactic Warriors enough to help him with the glitches.

He was equally interested in mine, wowing at the colors, styles, and sizes of the leaves I'd made. We quit his game and booted mine and he took over, using both the boy and the girl to catch leaves in a basket or rake them off the screen. Some of the leaves were drifting, but most were just falling straight down as though they were made of iron.

"Are you going to have one of them hit the other over the head with the rake?"

Not only was that a predictable question, it was a rerun, like some of Nanna's. "That would be your game, not mine."

"Have you thought of a name for it yet?"

"Not yet. Maybe I should call it Leaf Wars."

Brod raked in more leaves. We were both so good at playing these games that we had the highest scores on some of the games at the arcade at the mall.

"Everything checks out so far," he said, moving his eyes around and beyond the computer. We tried to remember that being so close and looking too long at a computer was not good for the eyes. "I see you have another peacock feather."

His noticing made me blush as if I had just openly confessed my love for Annajoy. Before I could answer I had to remind myself that peacock feathers couldn't be "read" as some people supposedly read tea leaves.

Then I said, "Oh, yeah," as if that feather I'd stuck in my pencil holder were the most casual peacock feather in the world.

For a distraction, for myself more than for him, I called his attention to the picture I'd pinned to the bulletin board of Nanna in scuba gear.

"What in the world is she doing?"

I told him about Nanna's onion-chopping method.

"Neat," he said. "Your Nanna is so funny."

And that brought us back to Nanna.

"Sometimes I just wish so much I could have had my grandparents." His voice was soft and he was usually tough and unsentimental. Whenever he'd spoken about his grand-parents before, he'd just sounded practical about it. So they'd died before he was born. He'd simply treated it as a fact, that's all.

I had always been glad I had Nanna, and my eyes stung at the thought of Dad's conversation with me in the attic a while ago.

"I've got some pictures of us with Nanna," I said, and I pulled the box of snapshots from under the bed and foraged through them.

"You still have that cake box?"

"You remember?"

"Sure I remember. Your Uncle Patrick gave you your camera for your eighth birthday and he took some pictures with it, and when you had them developed you put them in the cake box. How many people keep their snapshots in a cake box?"

I started tossing snapshots on the bed. Of Nanna, of me and Nanna, of us and Brod.

"Here," I said to Brod, handing him pictures of him when he was with me and Nanna at mini-golf, beach, water park. We both started laughing at one of him the first time he'd come down the biggest slide. For all his bravado he was looking a bit alarmed as he reached the bottom. Standing beside the pool, Nanna looked alarmed, too. I'd snapped both of them in mid-alarm.

"You thought you were going to drown," I said.

"I did not," he protested. Then he nodded and admitted, "Yes, I did."

"You did choke and sputter. I was about to come rescue

you and I think Nanna was, too, but you found your feet."

He grinned. "And I didn't drown."

"Nope. You didn't." I handed him several snapshots. "Here. You take a couple. She's been your Nanna, too."

# Chapter Six

A peacock feather was difficult to take to school secretly. Even if I wrapped it, I would get the question "What is it?" from everyone. I could say, "A kite." But whatever I did, people would notice that the strange, long, thin package changed hands from me to Annajoy. So I kept avoiding it. There were couples all over school. Apparently some people found this easy. I wasn't one of them.

Adam said that nothing else had happened with the KKK, no more threats, and Brod and I were stabilized at least, acting normal except for glaring at each other occasionally. Brod and Molo just left each other alone. Adam hadn't even decided on his project for the science fair yet and it was less than three weeks away.

Brod and I had decided to add an introduction to computers to our presentation and this was harder than programming. We were used to thinking in step-by-step increments, but that would be tedious for a quick introduction. On the other hand, we knew so much about computers it was hard for us to explain to people without immediately going over their heads. Lots of kids could walk up to the exhibit and just begin. But for those who weren't familiar with computer games, we wanted to make it easy and fun to play and enjoy. Especially girls. I thought it was terrible that computer and video games were so oriented to boys. I was surprised that Brod agreed with me on this, but his motive was only Annajoy. My motive was only partly Annajoy. I thought I wanted to do computer stuff for my career, fun, exciting, but peaceful games, like the songs Mom and Dad sang.

At school we had time together in the computer lab, and after school we used to take turns between our houses, but now I wanted to be home, to be near Nanna.

"It's not like she's just visiting," Brod said in complaint one day. "She's come to live with you. You'll have plenty of time to be with her and we have to get finished."

Brod knew that Nanna didn't quite know who he was, and he knew she'd done something totally uncharacteristic in getting the quail, but there was a lot I hadn't told him. He came over almost daily now, but we were mostly in my room except that we could take "Nanna breaks" and go be with her for short periods. We always stopped first to admire Janek, who was growing fast. Some of his adult feathers had already come into his wings. Janek was good for Nanna. She was most normal when she was with the bird. Maybe because when anyone came to her room to see Janek, they just talked about the quail and nothing else much came up.

I still wanted Brod to think this was the way Nanna was and that whatever strangeness he noticed was temporary. I wanted it to be temporary. Like why he'd attacked Molo, this was just another thing we hadn't told each other.

73

We stood in a long pause at the end of his driveway one day while I tried to convince myself to do computers at his house. We had the same kind of computer so all that was required was for us to bring our own game disks. My reluctance, I began to understand, was that I was no longer comfortable at Brod's house. His father worked odd hours and I never knew when he'd be there or when he'd come blustering in.

"I can't explain it," I said. "I just have to be with Nanna." I shrugged and Brod shrugged and we headed to our own houses.

I announced my arrival by swinging around the door frame into the kitchen.

Mom and Nanna were facing off.

Nanna had her hands on her hips and I could tell from Mom's expression it wasn't the first time they'd gone around the subject.

"What I want to know is, are you the manager here?" Nanna pounced on each word and left a space between. "Because I want to report a lost purse."

Behind Nanna's back I shook my head and grinned at Mom as I opened the refrigerator to grab my snack.

"The group of us went out to lunch and I left my purse at the restaurant and I can't get anyone to go see about it for me. If I knew the name of the restaurant, I'd call myself."

That was a new twist, I thought, her knowing where she'd left it. Soft drink and apple in my hand, I said, "Maybe I can help find it." I was mowed down with surly looks from both Mom and Nanna. Mom's was signaling me to butt out and Nanna told me with words.

"If it could be found, young man, I would have found it."

"Dad called the restaurant," Mom told me. "He even drove back over to look. The manager helped. No purse."

With tight lips Nanna said, "But I myself was not taken to look." She shrugged. "If it's not there, then I guess it was stolen."

"Sounds like it to me." I bit into the apple with a satisfying crunch. From the reruns I gathered that a thorough search had been made at home before Dad jaunted off to the restaurant. Apparently this time Nanna's purse was really gone.

"Dad and I are going to take her shopping for a replacement," Mom said. "You just stay around the house. I don't know how long we'll be."

"I don't want a new purse," Nanna said. "I want my old one back. I want it reported to the management, if I could ever find out who the management is." She glared at Mom. "And to the police. All my things were in it. Important things, my checkbook, my billfold with my driver's license and credit cards."

"Yes, Mother Vee, I know. And all that's being done." I knew Mom had said that thirteen times already. "I just thought you'd like to have a replacement until it is found."

"Well, I certainly would." Nanna raised herself three inches taller into what we called "one of her huffies." In the past we saw them rarely; now they were a regular part of our lives. "I've carried a purse all my life and my arm feels empty without it."

That was a truth. The way she hung onto that pocketbook, carrying it around from room to room even in the house, was proof enough she thought we were strangers. No wonder she didn't think it was safe to have her pocketbook out of her sight. And, thank goodness for small blessings, as Mom was fond of saying, she didn't know that her important things were no longer important. Dad had explained to me that even though she still had her actual driver's license, it had been canceled; likewise credit cards and her checkbook. Her bank account had been closed.

As far as we knew, no one had taken advantage of her, not even during the time she was lost. But she would be easy to take advantage of. When we took her out, she always wanted to pay for everything because she didn't want to take advantage of us.

Uncle Jim had told us several months ago that she was losing and misplacing money, even dropping it without noticing as she took it out of her billfold. It had been necessary for him to get something called power of attorney, which gave him the legal right to manage her affairs, including her money, which Dad had now.

Whenever she wanted money for something, Dad cashed one of her invalid checks and tried to make sure that she never had more than a few dollars in her pocketbook. When she worried about it, saying, "I don't have any money," he always assured her that she had her checkbook.

So now they were taking her to pick out a new pocketbook, so they could make up another fake purse and act like it was real. The thought of it gave me a pain under my rib cage. It was as though this person in our kitchen was a fake Nanna and the real Nanna's life was being closed down and canceled. No matter how crazy or foolish it was, I wanted her to have everything back: her bank account, her car, her house, her life.

I'd finished the apple and I pitched the core out the kitchen door for the birds and almost hit Dad, who was coming onto the deck from the studio. Except for when Nanna was in bed for the night, he and Mom no longer worked together in the studio. Dad hugged me as he passed, then hugged Nanna and kissed her cheek and slid his arm around Mom's waist and nuzzled her neck. Nanna smacked her lips as though she'd like to spit away his kiss. She didn't remember that she was the one who had taught him to be so loving and affectionate. The real Nanna believed in hugging, kissing, touching, and holding hands with everyone you cared about.

"I know you have things to do," he said to Mom. "So Mother and I are going to leave you, if you don't mind. We're going purse shopping."

"Well, I'm glad *someone* is taking me, since I don't have a car to take myself," Nanna said.

"John-too, want to come along?"

"Yeah, sure."

"Want to ask Broderick to come along?"

My mind reeled. Such a simple question, for which the answer had always been yes. I licked my lips and wavered between no, yes, no, yes.

"Well, you don't have to, you know. It's just a suggestion."

Just as he said that, I opted for yes. Mom knew of the difficulty, too, and they were both glad to see me and Brod making the effort for friendship. It was easier, I thought, for Brod to see Nanna more closely than for me to try to explain to Mom and Dad, or to myself.

I called to ask if Brod could come with us, and he could, pleased to join us and for a chance to get to the mall in range of the arcade. When Nanna was here before, she and I always used to jaunt off here and there and often included Brod. I guess he thought he knew why we hadn't since her arrival this time, and though there was truth to his reason, it wasn't the main reason.

"I want a white pocketbook for spring," Nanna said as we drove.

"It is spring, isn't it?" Dad said. I could tell he was as surprised and as pleased as I was that Nanna knew it was spring. Yesterday she'd said how warm it was for winter.

She watched out the window as eagerly as a child. Last summer, I remember, she began noticing and commenting on cows as if she'd never seen them before. Now it was white cars.

"You really dig white cars, don't you?" Brod commented after she'd pointed out several to us.

"Yes, I do. I've never seen such bright white, as though they'd been bleached. You know I don't have a car anymore, but I might get another one. If I do, I'll buy one of those white ones."

"What happened to your car?" Brod asked.

I gritted my teeth and gave him the elbow.

"They took it away. I thought everyone knew about that."

I rolled my eyeballs at Brod and he got the message. I should have told him. He shouldn't have had to be caught by surprise like this.

Dad pulled up at the back entrance where there was a place for the handicapped, with no curb. Brod and I jumped out and I opened the front door for Nanna. Inside, we waited on the nearest bench until Dad parked and came in. Brod was looking eagerly toward the arcade, which was near this back entrance. I guess they wanted to catch the kids at this point so they wouldn't go stringing up and down the mall, which they did, anyway, when their quarters ran out.

As soon as Dad came in he noticed where Brod was looking. "Now listen up, you guys. You know I wouldn't bring you out here without letting you have a crack at the arcade, and maybe you thought I'd leave you here while we do the errands, but all hands can be helpful for this trip. So first things first, okay?"

Brod and I okayed.

"Mother, this is a pretty big place," Dad said as we began our slow stroll. "How about a wheelchair to make it a bit easier?"

"I manage to get around perfectly well," Nanna said.

I could hear Nanna's interior dialogue. No ramps. No wheelchairs. We were near where parents checked out strollers for their babies, and Dad stopped and stepped up to the booth. I had never noticed they had wheelchairs. The wheelchair would eventually be free, but for now Dad paid a huge twenty-dollar deposit, which would be returned when the wheelchair was. Then the clerk unlocked a wheelchair.

Nanna was walking on.

"You boys just roll the chair along," Dad said, and when we caught up with Nanna, which was just a few steps, he said, "Mother, if you decide you want to ride in style, we won't have to go trotting back for it."

"If you like wasting your money that way." I did notice that this was one time Nanna wasn't offering to pay. "And one more thing. Just because I haven't seen my sons in years doesn't mean you to have to keep calling me Mother."

I thought Brod's eyes would pop out of his head and go

rolling down the mall. He snatched the wheelchair from me and found a clear space and began turning one-handed circles with the chair.

"Oh, it doesn't cost anything," Dad said, responding to the comment about the money and ignoring the one about calling her Mother. "You just have to pay a deposit in case you disappear with it, but it will be returned in full when we return with the chair."

"You might as well save yourself the trouble and return it right now," she said. "Unless you're going to use it yourself."

"Hey, John-too, give me a ride," Brod said, so we occupied ourselves by taking turns in the wheelchair. We were surprised at how easily it maneuvered. The small front wheels never stuck like the ones on a grocery store cart. Brod spun wheelies. I wondered if anyone really did just take off across the parking lot with a wheelchair as they did with grocery store carts.

Before we reached the long wings of the main mall, Nanna was looking for a place to sit.

"Well, Mrs. Viravek," Dad said, "we can sit on this bench or you can sit in the wheelchair, which may be a bit softer and has a back support."

With a rejecting look at the wheelchair she sat on the bench. "Thank you. 'Mrs. Viravek' is better than that Mother stuff."

Her response to Dad's jokingly calling her Mrs. Viravek pinched me inside somewhere. I knew she was having to adjust to a lot of things. So was I, but I would never call her Mrs. Viravek. She was Nanna and she'd just have to get used to it. "You might think about using the wheelchair just to sit on," he said as Brod and I continued our turns with it. "If only because it has a backrest."

Nanna studied the situation as she watched us play with the wheelchair. I had the feeling that she understood the wheelchair was for her and she didn't like us playing with it.

"Maybe it *would* be more comfortable sitting on something with a back."

I rolled the wheelchair up beside her, and Dad set the brake as though he did it every day. She struggled up and struggled down and I lifted her feet while Broderick flipped down the footrests.

In another minute Dad said, "Are you about ready to move on through the marvelously magnificent mall and find a new pocketbook? And would you rather walk or ride?"

I was interested in how Dad was choosing his words, making suggestions but giving her a choice. He certainly didn't think malls were marvelous, but he knew that anyone who was whatnot queen of the world had to be a first-class shopper.

Nanna moved to get up, then sat back and waved a hand. "I'm eighty years old. What does it matter? Just roll me along."

Brod and I looked at one another and grinned. I pushed first.

From previous experience we all thought we were in for a shopping siege. Nanna liked to look at everything and ponder a long time before she made a decision. There were jokes about how women loved to shop and Nanna fit the joke. Mom didn't.

We rolled into the first store Dad thought would have

pocketbooks and she spotted them immediately. "Over there," she directed. As soon as I had her in the vicinity she pointed and said, "That one."

It was on a rack she couldn't reach from the wheelchair and she didn't get up, so Dad handed it to her. I was expecting her to say, "No" or "Maybe" more times than usual but, no. She was firm in her decision. She found a purse she liked on the very first look.

"Nice," I said, stroking it. The "nice" wasn't for the purse but that she'd decided on one so quickly. It did feel good, though. White, soft leather. Her lost, strayed, or stolen one had been sort of a hard surface, navy blue. In my first memory of her she seemed to have zillions of purses with shoes to match. But for the past couple of years she'd been saying she was weeding out her things, and indeed she had. When Mom and Dad went to help her pack, she only had one pocketbook. The navy-blue one.

Next we went into a drugstore to replace the things she kept in her purse. Billfold, makeup, comb, tissues, emery boards, and all that paraphernalia. Dad was pushing now, and there was a wide aisle where everything but billfolds hung on racks. Dad stopped, set the brakes, and I lifted her feet while Brod flipped up the footrests so she could stand to reach what she wanted. Instead, she reached out from the chair.

"Just stand up and get whatever you want," Dad said.

Nanna made no attempt to get up.

"Take my arm if you like." I held out an arm.

Nanna didn't move to get up but was almost falling out of the chair stretching to reach, like Louis. I glanced at Dad.

He hunched a shoulder. "I'll push you closer so you can reach."

I was standing with my mouth open again. With her terrible forgettery, did she think sitting in a wheelchair meant she couldn't stand and walk? Or was she thinking, Okay, you wanted me in this chair and I'm staying in it?

When we had the "play purse" completed, she wanted to go look at pretty things, so for starters we went to the glassware section in a department store.

"What's that?" she asked, reaching out toward an aisle too narrow for the wheelchair.

"This store isn't handicapped-accessible," Brod said.

Dad said, "It certainly isn't."

Brod and I did the feet and flippers routine again, but she didn't move.

Again, she sat there reaching out like a baby.

"What is it you want?" Dad said. "I'll get it for you."

"That figurine. What is it?"

Dad picked it up and handed it to Nanna. It was a figurine of a boy and girl leaning into each other, gazing into one another's eyes.

"Me and Annajoy," Brod said as Nanna turned it in her hands.

"You wish," I said, thinking, No, me and Annajoy. I didn't think he'd made a move toward her yet, either, except that he did talk to her sometimes. I made up my mind that I was going to have to figure how to get that peacock feather off my desk.

"I guess I have enough things," she said at last. "Those shelves by the window are full."

"Well, Mother, you do have a lot of things. But of course you can have whatever you want."

Dad and I flashed eyes at one another and nearly rattled the glassware on the shelves shaking to contain our laughter. In Blairsville, she had had four or five times as many things on those shelves. Not to mention the yet-unopened boxes.

Brod had no idea what was so funny.

"Can we go back now?" she asked, as though we were the ones who were wearing her out with our shopping.

As we walked toward the arcade it struck me how Nanna's behavior affected my own. When she had reached out so much like a baby, I was overcome with the impulse to treat her like one. I had an overwhelming instinct to cup my hands under hers in case she dropped the figurine. I overcame it.

Nanna, who usually never passed a shop without at least looking in the window, was finished. She looked neither left nor right but just stared straight ahead.

Near the wheelchair stand, which was also near the arcade and the food court, Brod and I were freed.

"Watch out, now, look who's coming in," called a schoolmate who spotted us.

Dad had given us each two dollars, which we fed into the token machine. Brod headed for the war machines while I found the Tetris-like games that involved lining up and stacking columns of color blocks. My favorite game was an ego trip because not only did I have the highest score but the machine listed, in blinking lights, "High Score—John Viravek!"

When our tokens were gone and we came out, Dad gave us money for ice cream. "We've already had ours."

"I'd like another one," Nanna said. "I'll pay."

"What kind?" I asked, and we got it for her.

Dad got his refund for the wheelchair and we did the brake, feet, flipper trick, but Nanna just sat, looking blank, as though she didn't know this was the end of the ride.

"Here's where we return the wheelchair," I said. She looked back toward the main mall, forward toward the door, and she stretched out her arms for the door. I was swinging back and forth from laughter to near tears at a rapid pace.

"I'll go get the car," Dad said quickly. "You meet me at the door." He slapped the deposit back on the counter. "Please give it to my son when he brings the chair back." He walked briskly away while Brod and I, each with one hand on the wheelchair, strolled Nanna slowly to the door.

While Nanna was distracted over getting into the car, Brod said, "Now I get it. It's not just from the confusion of the move, is it? Why didn't you tell me?"

I shrugged.

"That's okay," he said. "Now I know."

# *Chapter Seven*

The science fair was in two weeks. In homeroom Ms. Johnson encouraged us to share what we were
doing for our science project. "If you don't know what
you're going to do, it's time to decide and get busy. Some
people have been working for weeks."

I refrained from laughing, refrained from looking at Adam,
but wondered if any ideas were stirring in his head yet. Brod
and I had known what we would do, and even been excused
from class to go to the computer lab to work on it long before
the dates for the science fair were announced. Whatever
grade you were in, the science fair happened every year. After
several people shared what their projects were I said that
Broderick Shaw and I were programming computer games.

"What a surprise," someone said.

"Computer games are for boys." That was Annajoy.
"They're too violent. Boys seem to like violence." *I* don't, I
wanted to say.

"Well, yes, a lot of the games are," I agreed. "But there are
a lot of good computer games, too. Chess and backgammon

and mini-golf, puzzles and color columns, Donkey Kong. Mine." I certainly couldn't risk saying "Falling Leaves" out loud in class. That was such a dumb, boring-sounding title it would cause me more trouble than letting them see me bring Annajoy a peacock feather.

"If it's not guns and war," Annajoy said, "it's symbolic bricks falling on symbolic heads. Or symbolic people or animals falling off symbolic cliffs. How many girls do you see in the arcade, anyway, unless they're just in there to hang around with the boys?"

A series of teasing and pleasurable hoots and catcalls rounded the room.

"Hey, yeah, Annajoy. Come watch me sometime."

"Hey, lighten up, Annajoy. They're just games. John-too, you need to make a Barbie Kong for the girls."

More hoots.

"Okay, people," Ms. Johnson interjected. "Let's have a little respect for everyone's point of view here."

"I'll bet Brod's is a battle game," Annajoy said. She was looking at me, and my feelings lurched. Between Nanna, Broderick, Adam, and Annajoy, interior lurching seemed to be happening a lot lately. Without even realizing I was doing it, I was looking back, wondering why she was paying this much attention to computer games. She caught my eye and smiled and I took a deep, hard breath and caught my lip in my teeth. Did she like me, too? As the class talked on about other projects, a smile slipped onto my face.

A loud whisper invaded. "Look at John-too and Annajoy." The smile fell right off and I faced front. So far I'd managed to be cool and not give any indication of how I felt about her.

Now I was about as cool as someone who'd spent too long in the sun at the beach.

I sat there considering changing my project to "How to Raise Rabbits," or something equally soft and furry.

"For my project, I'm hooking a rug," Adam said.

"This is a science project, Festivo, not the county fair."

"Well," said Ms. Johnson, "if any of you have an English assignment to write comedy, I think you could write about this discussion about science projects. But the bell is about to ring, so so long for today except for the ones I'll see in history later."

Adam and I moved into the hall shoulder-to-shoulder. "Funny bluff, Adam, so no one would know you hadn't even decided on a project yet."

"Like I said, I'm hooking a rug. Fibers that are not natural are made from chemicals, so that makes hooking a rug science, right? Natural fibers are science, too, unless you're going to be technical and call them agriculture."

"Or art. You'd better get with it. Surely you're going to use your photos in some way."

"What?"

"I mean, no, I don't mean *that* one." The very thought of that picture made me all flustered.

"I told you, I'm hooking a rug."

"Yeah, sure, my nephew the hooker."

The bell rang and we scampered into the classroom. Later, in history, I tried not to get caught gazing at Annajoy.

After school, as usual, Brod and I walked Adam to his bus. As soon as we continued without him Brod said, "You hear about Adam hooking a rug for the science fair?"

"Yeah." I laughed.

"He's a pansy as well as a spic."

I didn't say anything for about a half a minute. I was too stunned. "Okay, that's it, Brod. I've had it." I crossed the street right there instead of waiting until we got to Lover's Oak, so we walked home each on our own side of the street. Feelings lurching again. That was it. I couldn't stay friends with him anymore. But at the same time I felt the tremendous loss it would be.

Mom, Dad, and Nanna were all in the kitchen.

"Can we talk?" I said.

They understood instantly and Dad said, "Me or your mom?" And I understood they couldn't both be with me unless Nanna was in her room.

"Either one. Just somebody."

Dad said, "Claudi?" and Mom and I crossed the deck to the studio.

"You must really be upset about something, John-too. You didn't even get your snack."

Yes I was and no I hadn't. I hadn't spoken to Nanna, either.

"It's Broderick again. Last time Dad told you about it, this time you can tell him. I've been trying, I really have."

"Of course you have. That's been obvious, because he's been coming over again. You two seem to be getting along okay."

" 'Seem to' is right." I filled her in with what really happened before, Brod saying stupid things about Adam, and that now he'd done it again.

"Oh, sweetheart, that's a lot to handle. Especially when

you're having to also deal with things about Nanna. I guess life doesn't wait for us to get through one thing at a time. But it seems you are thinking things through carefully."

I shrugged. I was as weary as if I'd run four miles.

"Since you told Dad you'd never heard him make such remarks before, I wonder why he is now."

I shook my head and looked around the studio at all the familiar things. Piano, keyboard, guitar, banjo, mandolin. All the speakers and sound equipment. My parents practiced here and wrote songs here. Songs about love and peace and caring for people. "I can't believe how he could hide so much of himself from me."

"Well, certainly it's not because Adam and Edgardo have just come into the family. He's known Adam since all of you were seven. If he's always felt this way, he may have kept it to himself because he cares about you as a friend."

I was totally perplexed. It wasn't easy to even try to be objective.

"When people act out, it often comes from pain. Is Broderick in pain about something? Do you have any idea what?"

I shook my head and shrugged.

"Well, either that's not it or he's having a hard time over something he doesn't want to share with you."

Seemed as though there was a lot of not sharing going on between me and Brod.

"Do you think perhaps his father has these expectations of him, wanting Brod to share his feelings and opinions as we like for you to share ours?"

The idea was stunning. I felt a huge "Yes, of course," and my head gave a slow, tiny nod.

"If that's the case, then it doesn't even mean he really believes those things, just that it's easier to turn his anger toward you than toward his father. You may be close friends, but he doesn't have to live with you. I wish we could help you work this out. We care about Brod, too. He's almost like our boy, too."

"I hate him," I said. It felt wonderful and terrible and justified to hate him.

Mom hugged me. "Oh, I know. It's an absolutely normal reaction. But whether you remain friends or not I know you won't harbor the hate."

"Funny, I feel like harboring it." We'd been learning metaphors, similes, and irony in literature and I'd struggled to try to absorb what they meant and get them straight. Irony was seeping into my bones. Life was almost too ironic to bear.

"And I won't tell you what to do. But I think Broderick must need a friend very much right now."

I nearly spat. "He sure has a strange way of showing it."

Just like at the end of a fight, or the end of a round, anyway, a bell rang. It was the telephone. Mom raised a hand to indicate she wasn't going to answer. "Dad will get it." But we seemed to be finished. I couldn't get any more words out, or any more thinking, either. We sat in silence for several minutes, then she motioned toward the door. "Ready?"

We walked out arm in arm, back across the deck to the kitchen.

"Brod's waiting for you in your room," Dad said. "Is that all right?"

His words nearly knocked me down. How could he do this to me?

Mom said, "John."

"What is it? I'm sorry. I should have known what it was about when you said you needed to talk. So I'm slow. But I've got it now. You go on back out to the studio and I'll have him go on home."

I was seldom upset with my parents, but fury propelled me out of the kitchen, and I stormed down the hall and burst into my room.

"What are you doing here? How dare you?"

"Your dad invited me in and said I could wait in here."

I was absolutely dumbfounded that he could sit there looking so innocent.

"Well, you waited. Now you can go." Hand clinging to the doorknob, I stood aside to give him leaving room.

"I came to apologize," he said.

I took a long, deep breath and let it out slowly.

"Could you close the door, please?"

I felt my tongue protruding between my lips, like one of those silly dogs that go around with their tongues stuck out between their teeth. I got my tongue corralled behind my teeth and closed the door but didn't move from it.

"Would you come sit down instead of standing there glaring at me?"

Who was this? A penitent Broderick? Sure, I really believed that. I pulled the door closed and let go of the doorknob. At the desk I moved my chair back a bit from where he sat. I just couldn't sit as we usually did, both of us as close as we could get to the computer.

"I brought my game." He held up the disk.

I waited.

"I'm sorry. I can't talk about it."

92

On the "I'm sorry," my fury cycled down a bit, then roared back.

"You can't talk about it? That's an apology? You can't talk about it?"

Brod popped his disk into the disk drive and turned on my computer. He'd done this a million times. More than a hundred, anyway. But this time I felt ownership, that he shouldn't mess with my computer without asking.

The programming for Galactic Warriors came on-screen and he began studiously proofreading. Without any enthusiasm I let myself be drawn into it. In a couple of minutes he touched the Q, and when Galactic Warriors faded from the screen, he popped the disk out of the disk drive, pulled another disk from his pocket, and popped it in.

"You want to try something new?"

He had asked, but only after he had started it. My passion for computers piqued my interest in spite of myself, so I didn't stop him. When it came to screen, I wasn't too surprised to see the heading on the title bar: HOW TO DESTROY THE ENEMY. What now? A strange pleasure rippled through me. If he persisted in liking games like this, he wouldn't have a chance with Annajoy.

Brod just started playing the game. We both could take almost any game and figure it out without reading directions. For us it was easy. That's why it was hard to write out careful instructions for someone who didn't find it so easy. Like, maybe, Annajoy. With my Annajoy wanderings I missed the first part of the game, and when I paid attention, a dialogue box was on-screen.

Graphics of a train, train station, and crowds of little computer people filled the screen. The graphics were great, but as Brod began clicking on the people and putting them on the train, I wished *he* were on-screen so I could click him off. Apparently the more people you could get on the train, the better. Like my leaves, the people piled in and stacked up. He got forty-two in the car before the time was up. "If you get sixty in the car, the train starts moving down the track. You want to try?"

Brod started filling another car and got sixty figures of people in and the train began to move. Smoke puffed from the smokestack, the train whistle sounded, and the rods on the engine wheels moved as the wheels rolled, and there were sound effects of the train chugging down the track.

"Hey, that's neat," I said. I was entranced. I wasn't much of an artist yet, but I was a computer person and I thought it would be terrific to get into computer animation. The chugging and whistling train made me aware that I hadn't even put any sound effects in my game. I knew how to do it but had been concentrating so hard on the motions I hadn't even thought of sound. How would I make the scrape of a rake and the rattle of leaves? By recording myself scraping my throat? Or scraping a fork against . . . what?

"You want to try?" Brod asked again. He had returned the train to the station with all the people waiting outside.

I shrugged. Putting people on the train seemed harmless enough. I clicked and dragged and got the sixty people into the car and the train puffed and chugged its way down the track. I grinned at the feeling of satisfaction and power. I could move a train. Then it stopped and a dialogue box came up with other choices.

Brod took the mouse from me and clicked on a choice. "Bury them in a ditch."

Startled, I saw there was a long ditch beside the track, with the dirt piled along the edge.

"If you get them all in the ditch, the workmen shovel the dirt in over them."

"Bro-o-od. That's enough." The train had been so enchanting I forgot that the word "enemy" was in the game. "What is this?" I put my hand on the mouse and clicked back to the beginning, before the train station. A dialogue box with multiple-choice options came onto the screen.

> What can you do with a Jew?
> 1. Give them a ride on a railroad car.
> 2. Burn them in ovens.
> 3. Remove the gold from their teeth.
> 4. Bury them in a ditch.

I was too stunned to move or speak. This was a game about burying the Jews. Dad talked about things like this. I was ashamed, now, that I hadn't paid more attention to his stories about the "old country," Czechoslovakia. "Brod, why are you showing me this?"

Brod put his hand over mine and clicked the mouse for other options.

"Brod, I said enough." I reached across to press quit and he blocked me. I didn't want to see it but my brain and eye were too fast for my wishes.

In a tone so reasonable it was chilling, he said, "Let me show you this." The screen changed and another dialogue box appeared. Was he being innocent, brash, or mean?

What can you do to a nigger?

Or was he a racist and how come I never knew it?

Without reading the options I elbowed him hard, reached and turned off the power. He grabbed to stop me but was too late. The screen winked off and was dark. He put an armlock around my neck.

"If you've wrecked my disks you'll pay for it." Turning off the power instead of quitting the program with the power still on did sometimes damage a disk. It's what this one deserved.

"Three cents. I'll pay you three cents and they're not worth that much. How can you even look at this?" My stomach was cramping enough to make me cold and weak.

"It's worth a lot of money. It came from Germany."

And in the midst of the word game between us, he pressed the power button to turn it back on.

He still had me in the headlock, but I slid my hands up and under so suddenly it broke his hold, and I dove for the floor. He was on me in an instant but not before I pulled the plug.

"I don't want crap on my computer. I don't want it in my room. I don't want it in my house." I didn't want it in my head, but there it was, huge and stuck.

We were banging around under the desk and I figured he could trap me there forever if he wanted to. The little karate I'd learned didn't seem to offer many options from this position.

"No. You'd rather do something stupid like Falling Leaves," he said, crawling off me.

And there I was, peeping out from under the desk, when the door opened and Nanna stepped in.

"Do I hear fussing in here?"

"You sure do," Brod said. "He's messing up my disks."

One of the chairs had toppled. We must have made an awful racket and I didn't hear a bit of it.

Brod started to charge out of the room, but Nanna stood broadside in the doorway.

"Now, boys, let's just sit down and talk about it." She touched Brod on the shoulder. "What is this all about?"

I glared at Brod. "Sure, Brod. You tell her what this is all about."

"I told her already. You were messing up my disks." She had stepped farther into the room, thinking she would sit us down to talk it out. Brod stepped around her and stalked out.

"Well, then, you tell me what this was all about."

I shoved up from the floor, ready for her help and comfort. Was this my old Nanna back? I could tell her. I could tell her anything. My spirits rose a millimeter.

"If you won't talk to me," she said, and I thought I could hear the rest of her sentence, "then talk to your mother or father." But no. She said, "I'll have to report you to the management." My feelings hit the basement. This was the Nanna who didn't even know me. How could I possibly explain to her the hate that had entered this room with Brod's computer game? It even made me hate her.

# *Chapter Eight*

All weekend long, Nanna repeatedly complained to the management about "the boys fussing." Apparently it reran itself in her head the way we could have the computer return the train to the station and begin again. Mom and Dad took turns replying, "Children fuss sometimes."

"I had two boys, and they never fussed," Nanna insisted. "Of course, maybe they fuss now, but I wouldn't know. I haven't seen them in years."

She'd been here nearly six weeks now and she was settling in and getting familiar with the physical place, but we, who should be the most familiar to her, were new to her every day. When I tried to spend more time with her, I only managed to irritate her.

On Monday, heading out to school, I saw Brod waiting on the corner just like always. I did a quick U-turn and went the other way. Around the next corner I was instantly in foreign territory, which surprised me. Down to Brod's corner, up Albany, and through Lover's Oak was simply the shortest way to school and I'd never tried another. This street, named George after the man who was king when the colony of Georgia was founded, didn't go anywhere I ever went. Although it did go by the east end of school, I always came through the back gate even on those occasions when Mom or Dad dropped me off. Surely I had been down George Street in the car a time or two, but I knew for sure I'd never walked down it in my twelve years of being on earth in Hanover, Georgia.

There were kids on the street walking to school, but none I knew. It was as if I thought the world ended before this street. We didn't have gangs or territories but I was definitely out of mine. I recognized the names of the cross streets, as Hanover was an east-west, north-south sort of town, and I crossed the same streets I always crossed, just a block down. Suddenly I heard my name. It was almost as startling as an earthquake.

"Hey, John-too, what are you doing over this way?" It was Molo crossing a yard—his, I suppose—and carrying a trombone case.

"Oh, I just live down there, around the corner on Dartmouth. I usually walk down Albany."

"Oh, yeah, that makes sense." He fell in step with me.

"I didn't know you lived down here."

"All my life. I didn't know you lived down this way, either."

"All my life."

How weird that we had both set such narrow geographic limits on our world. "I forgot you were in band."

He laughed. "All my life."

"Nah," I said. "You don't start school band until sixth grade." A lot of my schoolmates had started last year.

"Well, not school band until last year, but I've had music in my life all my life. Everybody in my family plays something."

"Mine, too. I mean, I don't really play anything myself, but I've had music all my life, too."

"Yeah, your parents are folksingers. I know."

"You do?" It always surprised me when people knew about my parents. They weren't famous, like names everyone would recognize, John and Claudia Viravek, but they were pretty well known. I didn't think about them in those terms. They were just Mom and Dad.

Molo and I walked along chattering happily, as though we'd just discovered one another, which I guess we had. At the back of the school we veered left toward the back gate. A stream of students flowed through the gate and buses turned into the adjacent driveway to the bus circle. This kept school traffic off Princess Street, which was busy enough already. Even though I'd gone out of my way two blocks, there was Broderick, just coming up to the back gate. I wondered if he'd seen me make my U-turn or how long he had waited for me. I felt a pinch of guilt. I should have had the courage to at least call out to him and say, "Hey, I'm not walking with you anymore." Then when he saw me, and saw I was with Molo, I was peppered with guilt. He stopped in his tracks, didn't speak, didn't say anything smart-mouthed, just looked shocked and pale, as if all the feistiness had just gone out of him.

Adam stepped down from the school bus with his "Yo,

John-too," and then he stopped in his tracks, too, taking in Molo and looking beyond us. To Broderick, I guessed. "Yo, Molo," he added.

Now I felt Broderick looming behind me, prickled because of the way he looked and wondering if he'd jump me from behind. I wished I could pull Nanna's trick and simply make him disappear from my mind and the school yard. Then I thought of the hate game, How to Destroy the Enemy, and shivered again. Was I now his enemy?

"Hey, are you okay?" Molo asked.

I knew he was referring to me, but I dismissed it. "Yeah, sure, why wouldn't I be?"

After I put my books down in homeroom, I went next door to Mr. Hamlin's. As I walked past Brod, he said to me, "Don't even ask. I already did."

I asked anyway. Told Mr. Hamlin that Brod and I were having a problem and couldn't work together anymore.

"Well, as I told Brod, you know these spaces are already assigned, according to the space you said you'd need when you registered your project. There simply isn't room to squeeze anything else in. You can either attempt to be compatible or draw straws to see who stays out."

"But we're getting a grade for this," I said.

"And anyone who doesn't have an exhibit will get a zero."

Brod called from his desk, "And I'm not dropping out."

I thought I might and wondered what a zero would do to my average. For participating in the science fair we'd get a grade of a hundred, which would count as one quarter of our grades. It didn't matter whether you won or even got an honorable mention.

In the computer lab during science period there was no way I could avoid Broderick. Without exchanging a word we took separate turns at the computer and ignored one another in between. There was such a huge awkwardness that I couldn't even concentrate. All I could do was recheck the stuff I'd already checked. I didn't have a functioning brain for trying to work out things for the introduction or even think of better titles. It was a totally wasted period.

To avoid Brod after school I even went out the front door. This was as strange as walking down George Street this morning. This was my second year at Hanover Middle School and I had never come or gone from this front door. Because I was going a different way, I was thinking in a different way, too. I wasn't looking for Annajoy, and there she was, speaking to me.

"You don't usually go out this door, do you, John-too?"

I almost fell down the stairs. "Uh, no, I don't. I usually go out the back way." My heart was leaping. Annajoy didn't ride the school bus. That meant she lived within walking distance.

"Where are you going?" she asked, head tilted, looking right at me as she spoke. We were on the sidewalk then. If I usually went out the back way to go home, then it seemed stupid to say "Home," but I said it. She made nothing of it.

"Which way do you go?" She extended an arm indicating all directions except south.

I wanted to grab my arm back, but there it was, stuck out indicating east. It wouldn't have been one step farther to go around the west end of the school.

"See you tomorrow, then."

Before I could recuperate, she was crossing the street, north, in the midst of a crowd and under the direction of a police officer who had stopped traffic. I stood there and watched her go, knowing the guys who knew how to do this would have quickly said, "Whichever way you're going." Back down George Street I didn't see Molo. There was probably band practice, anyway. I trudged homeward with good and bad feelings mixing up inside. Broderick, Molo, Nanna, Annajoy. I wanted to block out the whole hate-game thing and pretend it never happened. Maybe it didn't. Maybe "the boys" never had that fuss and maybe Nanna was going to be okay. And maybe I was going to cry.

To shake this, I thought of Annajoy, the way she had talked to me. While those thoughts were tumbling, I had an absolutely fabulous idea. Since computers weren't "friendly" to her, perhaps I could persuade her to help me make the introduction clear and plain for people who didn't know computers. Perfect. I was going to be working with Brod as little as possible. I could call Annajoy or ask her at school. Calling seemed safer. If she refused and I got embarrassed, I'd rather do it from a distance. I'd call her.

I was practically skipping along, and suddenly there was Nanna just ahead of me. I must have been walking with my head in the clouds not to have seen her sooner.

"Nanna. What are you doing?"

"What does it look like I'm doing?"

We were a block and a half from home. The new white pocketbook dangled from her arm. Mom and Dad would have a fit. I was going to have a fit. The street was paved, but pebbly, not smooth. She could fall. Some fool could see her, weak and old, and yank the purse and knock her off balance so easily.

"Well, come on and walk me home." I reached out and

touched her arm and I should have known better by now. She popped my hand. The old Nanna would have taken my hand, but this "new" Nanna didn't like being touched by strangers. Probably the old Nanna hadn't, either, but I'd never been a stranger to her before.

She humphed and snorted. "Can't I even take a walk without a chaperone? Somebody watches me every minute. They sent you to spy on me, didn't they?"

"No, Nanna. I'm just on my way home from school." I tapped my books, as proof. "Nanna . . ." I started to try to convince her to come with me, but her jaw was set and she was walking on. The only good thing at the moment was that she couldn't walk fast and I could run fast. I took off for home, and was yelling when I banged open the door.

Mother must have been in the studio because it was Dad who responded in alarm. "John-too, what's wrong?"

"Nanna," I told him, sputtering, breathless. "Walking down George Street. She wouldn't come back with me."

"I thought she was on the porch. I just checked on her a minute ago." His words trailed after him as he hustled out the door.

I dropped my books and fell onto the floor and lay still, trying to let some of these things evaporate from me. Was it just a few minutes ago I was in ecstasy over Annajoy in front of the school and as I walked along the street? It seemed like days ago, weeks, years, never. So Nanna was out walking alone. She could get hurt. Or lost, as she had when she had driven away a couple of months ago. In trying to let her have as much freedom as possible, Mom had even had an identification bracelet made, but Nanna wouldn't wear it.

Suddenly I dismissed Nanna and jumped up. If I was going to call Annajoy, this was a good time, because no one was around to hear my end of the conversation. On the way to the phone I said yes, no, yes, no to myself, but I kept going. The worst thing she could say to me was no. That's what Mom or Dad said when they encouraged me to ask for what I wanted. I sucked in my stomach and looked up her number—how many Soos could there be in Hanover? As I dialed I was thinking she wouldn't be home and hoped she wasn't.

She was.

I stammered but got the question out.

She would like to help.

My heart shouted "Yippie" while I calmly thanked her and set up a time. My house? Tomorrow after school? Both my parents and my grandmother would be here. She could walk home with me and we would give her a ride back, or one of my parents could pick us up after school. She'd like to walk, she said. We hung up while she called her mother for permission.

The phone rang just as Dad and Nanna came in.

"Okay, it's all set from my side," Annajoy said.

"Great! I'll see you at school tomorrow, then."

In the living room I saw that Nanna was in one of her huffies. I hoped Annajoy wasn't. I had rather banged the phone down in my haste to see about Nanna. No, surely that was okay, since we'd already talked. Nanna plunked onto the sofa and Dad headed for the kitchen.

"They won't even let me take a walk," Nanna said with venom.

I grimaced in pain for her. I was just getting to the age

where I could come and go pretty freely as long as I let my parents know where I was going. In the next few years that freedom would increase and I couldn't imagine a time when it would ever stop. And here was my independent, traveling-fool grandmother whose limit now was the front porch.

I looked at her sitting sadly there and ran to my room for a quick shuffle through my snapshot box and grabbed several pictures of me and Nanna and the places we'd been.

I sat beside her on the sofa. "Look, Nanna, there we are at Coleman Creek, admiring rhododendron. You've had some great walks at Coleman Creek." When I looked at her, she was blankly staring across the room. She made no comment. I flipped through the pictures, talking about some of her favorite places and things. The wild white azaleas on the top of Wayah Bald. Amicalola Falls, De Soto Falls, any falls.

"That's a lot of water going over," I said as I showed her the pictures of us at the falls. That's what she always said, but she gave no reaction.

"You've had lots of wonderful walks in lots of great places. You'll just have to remember all those walks." Still not responding, it was as though she was lost inside herself somewhere.

Something clicked into my head about how Alzheimer's was affecting her. I didn't know that much about the brain, and from what I did know, scientists thought the brain had an infinite capacity. But what if it didn't? Maybe it was like a computer and there was a limit to the memory. Maybe Nanna's brain was full. In computer terms, "out of memory." Unless it was possible to get her new brain disks or a new microchip for the brain, there was no way to add new memory or to retrieve what was lost. The thought made me feel both better and worse.

Dad appeared in the doorway and leaned against the door frame, watching me show her pictures. I was going to stop. What was the point? I was beginning to realize these weren't Nanna's memories anymore, but mine. The next picture was of one of the most fun and crazy things we did. There were lots of places to get pizza, but she regularly drove us sixty mountain miles for our favorite pizza.

"Remember we used to drive to Cherokee just because Rosario's had the best pizza?" There was a picture of the two of us in front of Rosario's. Some kind stranger had taken it with my camera. I thought I would float. Nanna smiled.

"Oh, yes, I used to drive all the way to Cherokee for that good pizza. When I had a car, of course. I no longer have a car. They took it away from me and I don't know why because I never had an accident." She pointed to me in the picture. "But who is this boy?"

"That's me, Nanna."

"When did we ever go to Cherokee together? I just met you since I moved here and I haven't been to Cherokee since then. That was in the mountains, and I don't know where this is, but it's definitely not the mountains."

"You're sure right about that," I said. The only hill in Hanover was the River Bridge.

Nanna's expression changed and she pushed the snapshots away. Some of them fell to the floor. Dad gave me a sympathetic glance. None of us had been able to find the right balance with Nanna. It seemed difficult and rude to ask, "Where are you, Nanna? Who are we today?"

Just in time, Mom came in from the studio and said the magic words.

"Shall we go for a ride?"

"Yes," Dad said.

"Yes," I said.

Nanna, standing up faster than I thought she could, said, "Let me get my purse."

# Chapter Nine

I glanced around for her pocketbook, thinking it was there at her feet. It wasn't. If she had taken it to her room while I was gathering snapshots, she was quicker than I thought. I followed her to her room, to be companionable, to try to smooth these emotional roller coasters we kept having. I let her look for the purse while I stepped over to the box and chirped at Janek. I put my hand down and he hopped over and pecked at me to see if I was food.

"Are you the one who keeps putting that bird in my room?" Nanna asked.

"What?" I knew I had heard her right, but I still wondered.

"Someone keeps putting that bird in my room and I can't find out who's doing it."

Palms up, I raised my hands, arms, and shoulders.

"Well, if you find out who it is, please tell them that I don't want it. I have never had a pet, never liked them or wanted one, and I don't know why someone thinks I want one now just because I'm old." As she talked she looked for her pocketbook in the closet, in drawers, and under her pillow. Did she really sometimes put it under there? I wondered. The times I'd been in on the search I'd never thought to look under the pillow.

Quail and lost purse made me dizzy. "I'll meet you on the porch," I said, and I walked away and breathed a hunk of fresh air. Mom and Dad were standing on the porch.

"Nanna's better," I announced.

They looked at me with raised eyebrows.

"She's back to her old self. She doesn't want Janek. Doesn't want a pet. Says she's never had a pet and doesn't want one now."

Mom and Dad humphed and smiled, and here came Nanna, purse gripped in her hand. As we paraded toward the car, I thought I should take some pictures of her and the purse. Nanna dangling the purse from her arm everywhere, Nanna with it at her feet, everywhere, and the purse by itself wherever Nanna left it, say, in the bathroom. I could call it the Nanna's Purse Series. Adam would have already done it, I was sure. I laughed at the idea, but not until I was in the backseat with Nanna did I really *see* the purse.

"Nanna. Where'd you find your blue purse?"

"What purse? This is just the same old blue one I've always had."

At the word "blue" Dad whipped his head around, which caused Mom to shriek. He was about to run down one of our pine trees. He snapped his head forward and made a jerky but safe entrance into the street.

"Where is the white one?" Dad asked.

"What white one? Do you mean a white pocketbook? I don't have a white pocketbook. Why would I carry a white purse in winter, anyway?"

It was as though we had conspired to invent the whole business of the white purse. On our plane of reality there was a white purse. On hers there was not. Someone was in the twilight zone and she thought it was us. We were having a hard time of it trying to stop insisting on *our* reality. The doctor had told us we needed to stop trying to reason with a person who had lost the ability to reason. Easy to say.

Dad headed out over toward the river and the bridge. "Let's go to the Pirate's Place on Golden Isle for dinner, how about it?"

"Yes, good." Mom.

"Yeah." Me.

"Anywhere is fine with me," said Nanna. "But aren't the others coming?"

"Not this time." Dad said it so quickly and so smoothly I was proud of him.

"What will they do for dinner, then?" Nanna asked, concerned about them.

Mom turned around smiling. "They'll manage."

As we clacked across the mesh lift span on the bridge, I spotted the red-shouldered hawk flying below us and had a rare look at those red shoulders. "Look," I shouted, "the hawk. To the right almost below the bridge." Everyone looked and saw.

"That hawk is lucky for me," Nanna exclaimed.

"Yes," I said, and we both turned to look back at it even when the highway curved and we could no longer see it. I had almost said, "Me, too," because it did seem like my lucky hawk, too. But I was learning. Slowly, perhaps, but I understood she was claiming it as her own, personal, and nobody else's, lucky hawk.

The causeway to Golden Isle took us past marsh grasses and tidal pools and all kinds of shorebirds, flying, fishing, wading. As we all soaked it up, Mom turned in her seat and looked at Nanna.

"Mother Vee, with all the people who live at the house, how could we get them all in here, anyway?"

"Well, I think you need a bus. One of those little vans."

"How many people do you think live there? Can you name them?"

"Well, I haven't counted," Nanna said, "but aside from all the staff, help, and management, the one I like best is that nice Jim who takes me places. He's the sweetest thing. You." She leaned forward and touched Dad on the shoulder. "There are you two and at least two couples. One of them lives out there in the studio and they go around singing all the time."

Mom nodded.

Nanna referred to several boys, including the two who fussed and the one who wandered around taking pictures. With the tips of her thumbs and forefingers, she formed a circle and placed them around her eyes. "Did I show you the one he took of me wearing the scuba mask?"

We nodded and said she had.

"There is one man named John," she continued, gritting her teeth. "I don't know what it is about him, but I just can't stand him." She even glanced around to see if John was in the car with us. From her point of view, he was not.

I'd heard of eyes the size of saucers, but I think ours were the size of dinner plates.

"And you"—she swept a hand to indicate all of us. "Well, I'm embarrassed because I know you've told me your names.

Probably more than once. But I don't remember. I'm eighty years old and can't remember everything anymore."

"I'm Claudia," said Mom.

"I'm John-too," I said.

And Dad said, "I'm Jim."

We stopped for a sailboat at the bridge at Golden Isle. It was a flat, road-level bridge and nothing but small motors could get under. No freighters and only a rare shrimp boat came this way, but tall cruisers and sailboats did. This was the Intracoastal Waterway.

At Pirate's Place we were lucky and got a table by the window. This was one of our favorite places. With rivers and the ocean, it was one of the few restaurants in the area with a view of the water. We overlooked dunes and beach and waves. Shrimp boats sculled in the distance, nets lowered like angel wings. Sandpipers strutted, skimmers skimmed, gulls glided, and seven pelicans held an unswerving course north, in single file.

We gazed out and talked of the sea. When the server came to take our orders, Nanna asked for sweetened tea. I raised my hand to touch hers to remind her that she always drank unsweetened tea and used artificial sweetener, but I stopped myself. When the drinks arrived, Nanna immediately reached for the packet of sweetener.

"No, Nanna," I said. "You ordered sweetened tea."

"I never order sweetened tea," she said, tearing the packet open and dumping the powdery contents into her glass. She stirred, sipped, and laughed. "Well, I guess I had already put in some sweetener. I certainly have sweet now!"

The food arrived. Platters of steaming seafood. And at first bite, Nanna suddenly stared at Mom and said, "I don't like that hat."

"That's all right, Mother Vee. I won't try to make you wear it," Mom said, which was the same thing she'd said before when Nanna commented about the hat.

I thought it was pretty funny, and Dad and I smiled at each other because we delighted in Mom's hat.

Nanna popped a shrimp into her mouth, and when she had finished chewing, she said again, "I don't like that hat."

Mom laughed and repeated her statement.

Then, in between almost every bite, Nanna loudly announced her dislike of the hat. After several times, I felt people looking. I glanced at the nearby tables hoping it wasn't true, but it was. A few of them were looking amused, but my amusement was disappearing.

"Yeah, Nanna," I said. "We know you don't like Mom's hat. You don't have to tell us anymore."

Nanna raised herself into one of her huffies. "Do you mean I am not entitled to my opinion?"

"Of course you are," Dad said smoothly. "But now that you've expressed it, you don't have to keep repeating it."

"Well," she said, looking determined to be sure she *had* expressed her opinion, "I don't like that hat."

I wanted to stand up and shout at all the observers, "She's eighty years old. What does it matter?" But when I glanced around again, everyone was carefully not noticing. And I saw Annajoy. I gasped with pleasure and pain but, thank goodness, she was also not noticing.

I gripped my tea glass and sipped slowly so I could look over the rim of the glass at Annajoy. I thought I might walk over to say hello, but I knew I'd say hello and she'd say hello and I wouldn't be able to think of anything else to say, and I would just stand there feeling stupid, so I stayed put.

In the meantime, between every bite, Nanna made her five-word comment on the hat, with no variations on the theme, no incidentals. This was not a fugue, which had overlapping repetitions with small changes in every version.

"Are you counting the five hundred hats of Bartholomew Cubbins?" I asked. Mom and Dad chuckled.

"Five hundred hats?" Nanna looked around. "I only see one hat."

Over dessert, Mom and Dad abstaining, Nanna leaned forward toward Mom and said, "Well. Actually, it's not the hat I hate. It's you!"

Dad gasped.

In the huge silence I thought, Oh, a variation. A grace note. Or a lack of grace note.

Quite loudly Dad said, "Mother, you are so rude!"

Mouth hanging open in surprise, Mom looked back and forth from Dad to Nanna, skipping me.

"Are you telling me I'm not entitled to my opinion?"

"I'm telling you Claudi has never been anything but good to you. I can't believe you can be so hateful."

I caught Mom's glance, and she and I both put hands to our mouths to try to stop our snorting snickers. Dad and Nanna, who hated weapons, both had their emotional swords drawn, sharp and shiny. I thought there was a difference in what Nanna had said and what she actually meant. What I heard in my mind's understanding was, "It's not the hat I hate, but I don't like it on you." Which was different, if still not very nice.

Dad was caught up in defending Mom from the literal

meaning of the words, honing in on how sweet Mom had always been to Nanna. Nanna was drawn up taller than I'd ever seen her in the grip of an enormous huffy.

The people around us chattered busily among themselves, actively avoiding even the appearance of listening. Mom and I gave in to laughter until we were in spasms, and every time we were almost under control we made the mistake of glancing at one another and the near hysteria resumed.

When I thought I was about to truly get control of myself, Nanna sat up even straighter, raising her shoulders nearly to her ears. "Well, I'm glad *you* think it's so funny," and we were off again.

I had no tea left, but sipped, anyway, to glance over the rim at Annajoy.

She was noticing. She gave a small wave and a big smile.

Even so, I wanted to slither under the table and disappear or, at the very least, make a quick escape. I was careful not to look at Annajoy as we made our way out. And Nanna didn't say another word about the hat.

# Chapter Ten

Another walk to school with Molo, George Street a bit more familiar than it had been yesterday.

We talked about music. We talked about the science fair. He was doing a project about one-celled animals, the microscopic creatures that live in a drop of water.

"Aren't you friends with Broderick anymore?" he asked.

"Nah. I guess not." Strange, though, walking in step with Molo instead of Brod.

"Well, in spite of what he did to me, I'm sorry. You two have been tight ever since I can remember."

"I just never noticed that he was such a jerk." Such a prejudiced jerk, I thought, but did not say it. "Since you brought up the subject, what did you do to set him off, anyway?"

"Hey, nothing, man, not one thing. We've always gotten along okay. He must have just been in the mood to jump someone. You know how he is."

Yeah. I knew. More than I wanted to know, more than I would ever tell Molo.

"He's lucky he chose me, that's all I can say."

"Why is that?" I was learning how to take long strides, keeping pace with him.

"Because my parents have raised me to be seriously nonviolent, like Dr. Martin Luther King."

"Yeah, me, too. We have a lot in common."

"Yeah, I didn't miss that crack about you should design a computer game called Barbie Kong because you don't like the kill-kill-kill games. What is your game, anyway?"

I told him about it, but even with him I didn't tell him the title.

At school I met Adam at the bus, though I was instantly distracted. Even though I knew, now, that she came and went from the front door, I was looking for Annajoy. Inside, though, there she was, coming from the opposite end of the hall. She came straight at me.

"John-too, I want you to know it's okay about your Nanna."

She had indeed noticed. Who in the whole place could have missed it?

"No need to be embarrassed. I know she can't help it. My great-grandmother is like that, too."

Standing here beside Annajoy, I felt myself going red as a radish.

"Thanks," I said.

When Annajoy had gone on, preceding us, Adam asked, with great interest, "What was that about?" We were going to the same homeroom and I felt like a dunce not just walking along with her. I told Adam about Nanna and the hat. Then, acting as though it were the most ordinary thing in the world,

I told him that Annajoy would be helping me with the introduction part of my project.

"Mmmmm," he said. "Mmmmm."

I could scarcely believe that Annajoy really would come home with me after school, but there we were, walking along together, talking about school and the science fair and the weather, just like friends.

Mom, Dad, and Nanna were on the porch. I introduced them to Annajoy.

"Yes, I think I've met you before," Nanna said.

"Nanna likes to sit out here and bird-watch," I said, to cover her statement.

"Oh, yes," Nanna said, describing the birds flying from here to there and there to here.

"She has a bird in her room, too," I said. "Nanna, will you show us Janek?"

"Who keeps putting that bird in my room?" she asked, getting up and walking to the door, anyway.

In her bedroom I had to urge her to put her hand down, but when she did Janek hopped right into it, like always. Annajoy was charmed. And, for a moment, Nanna was, too.

"Annajoy is going to help me with my project for the science fair," I said.

"Could you use a bird?"

I laughed and wanted to hug her, but I didn't want any ruffles in front of Annajoy.

"Your Nanna's sweet," Annajoy said on the way to my room.

"Yes. She is."

First I showed her my game and was thrilled that she liked it. Or said she did, and I didn't figure Annajoy for a faker.

"I'm having a problem with the title. Falling Leaves doesn't sound very exciting."

Knowing very little about computers, she astonished me by saying, "Could you have the leaves form a shape as they pile up? Maybe make the shape of a larger leaf?"

"Yes, I could. What a great idea." I thought immediately of a heart.

"Could you make them build up like, maybe, an eagle? The leaves fall down and then gather into the shape of a bird and fly away?"

"A hawk." And as often happens, other ideas came roaring out. "A phoenix! The pile of leaves could burst into flames and a phoenix would rise from the ashes."

"John-too, that's great."

It was not possible to make such a change in time for the science fair, but I knew I would do it later. Hawk or phoenix.

"Transmigration?" she said.

"Metamorphosis?"

"Osmosis?"

Those terms we were just learning and obviously we didn't have them straight yet. I nearly fell out of my chair with the pleasure of laughing with Annajoy.

"I might not have time to rearrange my program to make a shape," I told her. "But if I did, what about a castle? Castles are popular."

"With a knight and a princess raking leaves?"

"Both! If I only had more time. I'm beginning to see I could make this one game into a lifetime project, but for the moment Dick and Jane will have to rake the leaves."

"You call them Dick and Jane?" Our laughter was glorious.

I had to bite my lip, like pinching myself, to see if this was real.

"What about a tree? Could you have a tree shedding its leaves, and then as they pile up, the leaves can turn back into a tree ready for the next game?"

"Great idea. I like that. I could call it Timber Trash." I could see she didn't get it. "Leaves. The trash from trees."

"Oh."

I smiled and shrugged. "Takes the punch out of it if you have to explain the joke."

"Oh, I'm sorry," she said, and I very nearly reached out to take her hand and scared myself silly with the very idea.

I distracted us by showing her the business at hand with the introduction. She read through what Brod and I had done so far and it did not make sense to her. But instantly she was involved and began telling me what was not clear.

"I don't understand that," she said, or, "That's confusing." And bit by bit we made the introduction totally understandable even to someone who had never touched the keyboard of a computer before. Even to Nanna. Well, no, maybe not. I was almost giddy. It was great just to be with Annajoy and also pure fun to share ideas and work out solutions. As Brod and I always had.

When we were almost done, we got awkward with one another. Maybe she almost reached out for my hand and scared herself. She started looking around my room and she spotted the picture of Nanna in the scuba mask. I explained and we laughed again. It was nice to know that Annajoy was a laughing sort of girl.

I saw the peacock feather and picked it up.

"Ohhh, it's beautiful."

"It's yours."

"You mean it?"

I started to say I could get all I wanted, but I realized that would take away from the gift, so I told the real truth.

"Believe it or not, I got it for you. I just didn't know how to give it to you."

"You just give it, silly." She brushed the feather across her cheek and her hair and said a long-drawn-out "Tha-a-anks."

Mom took her home and we all sat in the front seat, with Annajoy in the middle holding the peacock feather. At her house, I jumped up to let her out. I rode home with Mom, of course, but I didn't have to. I could have flown.

All week Nanna kept asking Mom and Dad, the staff, help, and management and me, "Do you know who keeps putting that quail in my room?"

At school Annajoy and I gave each other secret, special looks. I thought about her constantly and hoped she was thinking about me, too. I guess we didn't want to open this up to teasing.

Adam did ask, "How did it go with Annajoy?" and I allowed myself to say, "G-reat!"

Working Tuesday night and Wednesday afternoon and night, I designed and programmed a nifty castle. The leaves, after piling up above Dick's and Jane's heads, turned into a stone castle. I had decided on Kingdom of Leaves for a title and hoped people would be curious enough about a "Kingdom of Leaves" to want to try the game.

On Thursday, the day before the science fair, Mom and Dad were sitting on the porch swing keeping watch on the world.

As I plunked into the rocking chair, I automatically asked, "Where's Nanna?"

"Taking a nap," Mom said. "We are sitting here wondering why we have been so knuckleheaded about that quail. Why did we think she would remember that she adored this quail? She will never remember that it was she, herself, who wanted it in the first place. We don't seem to be getting any better at understanding her."

Dad pressed his foot to the porch floor to keep the swing in motion, and I matched my rock to their swing. "The first time she said something I should have simply taken it out of her room and let it disappear, like we did the boxes."

The boxes were so long ago I scarcely recalled them, hadn't looked at them since we took them to the attic or given them any more thought than Nanna had.

"Pardon the bad pun, but when Mother wakes up, we're going to kill two birds with one stone. We will take Nanna for a ride and return poor Janek to the game farm."

"I'll give them a call," Mom said.

As she left the porch, Dad asked how things were with Brod.

"They're not."

"I thought so, since you're still walking down George Street." He swung and I rocked. "Are you ready for the science fair?"

"Oh, yeah. We've been working in the computer lab during science class. Other than that, we're pretty much avoiding each other. We're ready, though I'd rather be sick."

"That's too bad. Not fun to be disappointed by a friend, eh? And I know how much you've looked forward to this." Push, swing. Push, rock. "So, things worked out well with Annajoy, then?"

"Oh, yeah." Funny how quickly a mood can change sometimes.

"Do I detect some interest in Annajoy other than scientific?"

I tried without success to keep from grinning all over myself and finally said, "Oh, yeah. I mean, I think so. Or I mean I know so from my point of view. I'm just not sure about hers." But, strangely enough, I was. I saw our whole lives together. Junior high, high school, college, marriage, children, careers, the whole thing. But I'd keep this thought to myself.

"Well, it sounds as if all is not glum."

Mom returned to say we were invited for dinner at eight o'clock. I was thinking about how neat Dad was, not reminding me of what he'd said about staying friends with Brod, not teasing me about Annajoy.

"Mention of dinner reminds me I haven't made my regular raid on the refrigerator." They laughed as I headed for the door. I scooped up some grub and carried it to my room, clicked on the computer to go over my program one last time. It was perfect. I knew it was perfect, but I still had the compulsion to check it with Brod one more time. I dismissed it. I'd added sound effects and now the rake scraped and the leaves rattled against the basket. At school Brod and I had copied all the programs onto the same disk and made us each a copy. I didn't look at Brod's game again and, at school, anyway, he didn't look at mine. As far as I knew he didn't know why I'd renamed it Kingdom of Leaves.

When I came out of my room, the box with Janek was in the corner of the kitchen and Nanna was in the dining room making tsking sounds in disgust over having a bird in the house. This I understood. The old Nanna had never liked pets. But I would miss Janek. I sat with her, quietly, hoping this return to her old self meant, also, a turning away from the problems she had been having.

She was looking at the whatnot shelf, so I looked, too. After all these weeks she'd finally put some of her things on it.

"Hey, great, Nanna. They look great."

Standing up, she walked over and fingered the things on the shelf.

"Who put these here?" she demanded. One by one she picked up each item, examined it, and either returned it to the shelf or set it on the dining table. There was a selection of her favorite things, hand-painted china plates, egg art as lovely as the famous Fabergé eggs but not with real jewels, several bells, figurines and paperweights.

"I thought you might like to have a few of your things set out," Mom said, coming in from the kitchen.

Nanna reached out and patted the edge of the shelf unit. "Some of these aren't mine. And I hate shelves that are cluttered with too many things."

Mom and I glanced at each other in surprise.

So much for returning to her old self. The old Nanna had that shelf stuffed with four times the number of things Mom had set out. She was not recovering from her recent problems. I didn't open my mouth, but I was thinking, "Where are you, Nanna, and who are you today?"

Picking up a plate and then an egg, turning each in her hands, she said, "I've done a lot of things in my life."

At least she knew she had made these things. They weren't squash casserole.

"Yes, Nanna," I said. "You have." I wanted to run and bring some more snapshots to help her remember things we'd done, to help her remember herself, but I didn't. If she was really getting better, returning to her old self, I had plenty of time. If she wasn't, well, I was beginning to catch on that most of the memories I shared with her were only mine now.

At seven-thirty Dad put the box with Janek in the trunk, and when we were in the car we could hear him chirping.

"Must we even take that bird when we go out?"

"We're taking it to the bird zoo, Nanna," I said. "We're having dinner out there with the rest of the family."

"Aren't the others coming?"

This time there was no hawk.

Edgardo and Patrick immediately took over the Janek box, Edgardo carrying it through the common room and out the back.

"I want to go," Nanna said. "I want to see the birds."

"Okay, let's go," I said, so happy she understood where she was. Both at home and in the car we had said where we were going, of course, but as we well knew she could forget in an instant.

"Where's Adam?" I asked as I started out with Nanna.

"Out there somewhere. You'll see him in a minute because he was watching for you," Rosie said.

Mom and Dad had both gone into Iris's kitchen, where dinner was being prepared. The separate kitchens were the first rooms on each side of the common room, so they could easily serve meals in the common room as well as separately on their own sides.

Nanna talked to the peacocks as she walked along, but none of them displayed the fantail for us. A few of the birds in the pens were beginning to roost, though it was still daylight. Edgardo and Patrick had released Janek in the quail pen, and already I couldn't pick him out from the bevy of young quail. There were dozens about the same size, just a few weeks from the table, oily wing feathers shining against the remaining down.

"Where are they going now?" Nanna asked as Edgardo and Patrick walked away toward the hatching shed. She was already following. Adam came racing up on the ATV and slowed down to a creep as he kept pace with us.

"That's a noisy thing," Nanna said.

Adam gunned it to emphasize the sound.

Nanna covered her ears, and at the hatching shed, where my two brothers-in-law had disappeared, she tugged at the door and stepped inside. As almost always, there was the immediate sound of the hatching dance and Nanna was as riveted by it as she had been those few weeks earlier when she came home with Janek.

"What's happening?" Nanna asked. "Are they hatching?"

Edgardo and Patrick answered her questions as though they had never been asked before, telling her how the hatching chick pecked the inside of the egg. When one hatched, Nanna oohed and ahhed and wanted one. I yanked at Adam's sleeve and we left Edgardo and Patrick with the problem.

"She wants another one?" Adam was as disbelieving as I was.

We roared around the ATV track, stopping along the way at some of our favorite places. The gator was lolling on the bank and slid into the water at our approach. It was about four and a half feet, about six inches bigger than last year.

"I guess it knows we're still bigger than it is," Adam said. Across the inland marsh where Adam had seen the Ku Klux Klanners, some people were having a picnic. Just a normal evening, like nothing unusual ever happened there. When we walked out near the owl's roost, Adam said, "So, okay, what's this Annajoy business?"

Even in the cool evening air I could feel myself go red again. "Well, Adam, my man. I guess this Annajoy business is that I have my first real girlfriend."

He didn't act surprised.

As soon as we walked back in the house the smells of dinner reached us. Dad, Iris, and Patrick carried plates of green beans and potatoes and squash to the table in the common room. Mom was playing with Louis and I stepped in and took over. I didn't hear a quail peeping, so I guessed Edgardo and Patrick had not brought back a box with a new baby quail. Nanna didn't mention it and seemed at ease and perfectly happy. I was, too.

As we sat around the big table at a south-facing window, and watched the sky turn peach and pink in the gathering dusk, Louis entertained us and the talk was quiet, murmuring and lingering. Too lingering for me and Adam. We wolfed our food in as mannerly a fashion as we could manage, and Adam released us from the table by offering to show me his exhibit.

"Oh, you mean I get to see the hooked rug at last?"

We dashed off to the Festivo side of the house, and to my surprise, he really did have a project and a hooked "rug." I laughed. Sections of a diorama covered the floor and I walked carefully among them. A sign, MARSH AND WET WOODLANDS, announced the topic. End clippings from various trees were being kept moist in a sealed plastic storage box.

"Adam, this is fantastic!" With short pieces of yarn in variegated greens, golds, and browns he had created a marsh. He'd left places bare for the meandering creek and the mud-flats. He had a jar of real marsh mud to use tomorrow to complete the creation of the mudflats, and curving pieces of muddy blue-brown felt were ready to set into place for the creek. He also had some tiny birds and animals including an alligator to perch on the bank.

He had several sheets of paper mounted on cardboard illustrating and telling about the life cycle of the marsh, that marshlands were nature's nursery, and so on. We thumbed through them and also the series of photos he was using for the backdrop.

"I would have loved to have one of a diving hawk."

"Well, in order to do that you've got to get out there and watch."

"Yeah, well, it's too late now."

I told him my idea for flames and a phoenix, for which it was also too late. "Adam, wow. This is great. And you didn't share one bit of it with me."

"I didn't know how far I'd get with it."

I was overwhelmed with the details of his project. I got him in a light headlock. "What a great surprise. I'm so proud of my little nephew."

"I'll little-nephew you," he said, poking me in the ribs. "And," returning his attention to his project, "I thought I'd use this photo, too." He slid it in behind where some trees would border the edge of the far side of the marsh.

"Adam, no!" My adrenaline leaped and I almost leaped, too. It was the photo of the people in hoods and white robes.

"Gotcha," he said, removing the picture.

I said, "Whew!" What we didn't need was something like that at the science fair.

As we migrated back toward the common room, we sensed some soundless disturbance out front. A flicker of light.

"The woods are on fire," Adam shouted as we ran into the big room. Edgardo and Patrick and Dad were already crossing to the front window.

"¡Dios mio!" Edgardo said. "It's the Klan." We all ran and crowded at the window. In a spiel of Spanish, Edgardo told us to get down and he even stretched out arm and hand to push us back and down. Not just me and Adam but everyone, Dad and Mom, Rosie, Iris, Nanna and Patrick, too. "I never thought they'd really do anything."

All but Nanna dropped and huddled below the rim of the windowsills. Nanna's knees wouldn't let her duck or huddle. She stood to the side peeping out the window. What I saw was already imprinted in my eyes. A number of torches reflected off white-robed men. A couple of men grappled with something, or each other, at the edge of the yard.

I peeked out and counted. Eight torches, then two others

just lighting up. Ten. In the movies or on television such scenes had scared me, but right here, in live action, right in front of my eyes—"astonishing" and "terrifying" were not strong enough words.

Mom said, "They're going to burn a cross."

"They're what?" That was Nanna, looking over my head in full view of the window and not standing aside at all.

"Nanna, get down." I yanked on her shirttail.

"I'll call the police," Dad said, making a stooped waddle across the room to the phone.

"The baby!" Iris exclaimed, doing the same hunched scamper toward the open door to the side of the house, with Patrick waddling right behind.

Before we knew she'd left the window, Nanna had opened the door and started shouting. "You get away from here. We're not afraid of you."

"Nanna, no!" I said.

Mom, then Rosie, whisper-shouted their nos, but Nanna ignored us all and walked right out.

"Stay down," Edgardo said, cupping a hand behind Adam's and my heads to hold us there. "They could have guns."

Guns? Nanna disappeared from the doorway, and with calls of "No" at my back I ducked away from Edgardo's hand and crouched my way to the door. Backlighted by the fire from the torches, the silhouette of Nanna hobbled down the stairs.

"Nanna!" I said louder than I intended, and the word traveled out through the dark, and the dark eye holes in the white hoods turned toward us. A huge *"Shhhh"* issued from the window.

At the bottom of the stairs Nanna went down and I leaped from my crouch and bolted to her. But she hadn't fallen; she had picked up the garden hose and was turning the faucet.

"No!" I shouted fiercely, but she stood up and tottered her way down the pine-straw walkway with an arc of water before her. I jumped to bring her back.

"You get your hateful selves away from here," she shouted, showering the men with a stream of water. One of them set his torch to the cross, which sprang into flame. The stream of water did not prevail against it.

"Lady, you get on back in the house before you get hurt," called one of the ghostly men, moving toward her.

"I'm eighty years old. What does it matter?" She continued moving toward him until she was dousing him. His torch dimmed but roared back into flame.

"Lady," the man warned, but she kept tottering forward, splashing as many of them as the water would reach. I realized I had a fistful of her shirt, trying to hold her back or hiding behind her. I wasn't sure which.

"Get on out of here!" she shouted, following them to the full extent of the hose, and Edgardo followed even further, spraying them with a spurt of Spanish.

"The police are on the way," Dad said quietly. I didn't even know when the others had come out.

Nanna stood glaring after them, an arc of water spilling into the driveway.

"Here, Nanna, let me," Adam said, taking the hose from her and turning it onto the fiery cross. Soon we all stood in the dark hugging Nanna, saying she had scared us half to death.

"Nanna, you're a hero," Adam said, and everyone agreed.

"Oh, posh, hero," she said. "I'm eighty years old . . ."

We all chorused, "What does it matter?" and Nanna looked surprised that we knew what she was going to say.

Patrick came running down the driveway chanting a number, with two police cars right behind. "I have a description of the truck including the license number. I slipped through the woods to take a look. Write it down before I forget."

They did.

The police repeated our refrain to Nanna, that she was a hero, that she could have been hurt. And she repeated her refrain to them. "I'm eighty years old. What does it matter?"

"It matters to us," they said.

Edgardo said something quietly to the police, then trotted into the house and returned with what looked like a couple of letters. We all gathered around to see and hear.

Iris appeared in the doorway, cuddling Louis.

"We didn't tell you," he said, glancing at Rosie and Iris. "We didn't want to worry you. But now . . ." He handed the envelopes to one of the officers, who looked at them by flashlight and handed them to the other officers. They were at the bottom of the steps and I hopped to the porch so I could look over their shoulders. I already knew it was the threats Adam had told me about.

The first line read, "What do you do with a spic?"

I howled in pain.

"John-too, what is it?" Dad asked, curling an arm around me. "Are you okay?"

"Yes. No. I don't know." I couldn't tell the police what I was thinking. Besides, Brod's father didn't have a pickup truck. That was only a momentary relief. Anyone could get a ride with anyone. Finally I said, "I'll tell you later."

"Does it have anything to do with this?" He swept his free arm to include us and the shadow of the charred cross.

I shrugged.

"If it does, perhaps you should tell us now while the police are here."

So, feeling like a miserable traitor toward my lifelong friend, I told them about the hate game.

In the car on the way home I left my seat belt off so I could lean forward on the back of the front seat. Nanna fell asleep while I whispered and told Mom and Dad some of the details.

# *Chapter Eleven*

~~In the morning, both Mom and Dad came to wake me. I didn't have the heart for school or the long-awaited science fair. Last night had turned out all right: no one was hurt and Nanna was brave and funny. But after my horrible confession I didn't want to see Brod.

"I don't want to go," I muttered, and pulled the cover back over my head and burrowed. I wished I were a quail inside an egg and that it was a long time before I had to hatch.

"Blueberry pancakes," Dad said.

"Come on, get up and let's talk about it," Mom said, and together they rubbed my back and shoulders, which felt so good I just wanted to burrow deeper. But I got up and pulled on some clothes.

At the table they told me that Adam was already on the way to school. "Rosie and Edgardo are driving him to take his science fair exhibit. They wouldn't have wanted him to go on the bus today, anyway. They gave him the option of staying home or going to school and we give you the same option."

We each put another bite of pancakes in our mouths, but

I could feel other words lurking behind their pancakes, waiting to be said. They were.

"You can't let people like that have any control over your life, sweetheart," Dad said.

"Our recommendation is that you go on to school and act as normal as possible. If something happens that's too difficult, call us and we'll come get you."

"And when you're ready to go, we'll take you, if you'd like."

"I'd like it," I said, taking a swallow of milk. There's nothing better than cold milk with pancakes. "Does that mean everybody knows about it?"

"Well, yes. Anyone who's listened to the news."

I let out a long stream of air. "I feel terrible about Brod. Like a traitor. And I don't understand why I feel that way. He's the one who had the hate game. He's the one who jumped Molo and said terrible things about Adam." I pushed my plate back and sank onto my arms on the table. A hand rubbed the back of my head. From the left. Mom.

"Most people have a terrible time even thinking about it, much less talking about it, when someone they care about is acting badly. I imagine Broderick has some of those kinds of problems with and about his father."

Now Dad. "I don't know why we should expect you to understand, at age twelve, what most of the adults in the world don't understand, but most people say and do hateful things out of pain. The better people feel about themselves, the kinder they are able to be toward others."

Then Mom again. "That's why you are always so kind to people."

I burst out with a huge "Hah!"

If it had been on the news, Adam would take the brunt of the curiosity and the questions.

When I started to make my lunch, Mom handed it to me already made. Sometimes such a tiny thing as lunch is a gift. Usually I bought lunch at school but today everyone was bringing lunch. The cafeteria was entirely taken up by the science fair.

I slid my computer disk into my science book and against house rules I peeked into Nanna's room. I don't know what I thought might have happened to her in the night, the torch raiders coming and taking her out the window, or what. The opening of the door disturbed her and she opened one eye. I blew her a kiss and retreated without bothering her further, without knowing if she knew who I was today.

On the way to school we passed Brod. Dad honked and waved but didn't stop to offer a ride. He looked so alone, walking by himself, our poster rolled up and curled in one arm. Even in the car with my parents I felt alone, too.

"You have to come to school to see Adam's project," I told my parents as I got out of the car. "It's terrific. You'll be so amazed."

"We'll be there."

I checked into homeroom as we were supposed to do, left my books, took the disk, and walked through the busy hallways to the cafeteria to set up. Those who needed more time setting up, like Adam, had come early. We were to be ready to go by first period and we had first period to host the exhibits and walk around looking at the others. Beginning with second period, parents and other grades would start coming. Judging would be fourth period.

Our setup was easy. We both had single disks with our two

games and the introduction, which was on-screen and also on a poster. We'd done some neat introductory graphics including a last-minute segment called "Learn More About Computers," which explained what each component of a computer system was and what it did. As I wandered across the huge space toward our assigned area, I came directly to Adam, though I hadn't known where his area was. With all the sections of his Marsh and Wet Woodlands exhibit pushed together and the photos in the background, it was even more impressive than it had been last night.

"You okay?" he asked. We touched shoulders, elbows, hips, and hands in one of our greeting rituals.

"That was wild, wasn't it? But, yeah, I'm fine."

"Did you see the astronomy project?" Adam asked.

I wondered if he was really that cool about what had happened last night or whether he just wanted to avoid the subject.

"It has all the planets rotating and a background of stars with diagrams pointing out some of the constellations."

In an attempt at a feeble joke I said, "You've seen one planet, you've seen them all." Glancing down the aisle, ready to head on to my place, I saw Annajoy. She was standing by a display of moving planets. It was bright and colorful and attracted attention. I was glad I hadn't made my stupid remark too loudly. I didn't think she had heard.

"Ahhh," I said to Adam. "I get it. Thanks."

My next stop was by the stars and planets exhibit, of course. "Great exhibit," I said, though I felt like an absolute idiot. In the little time she helped me with making our introduction user-friendly I had not once asked what her project was.

"I want to apologize. I never even asked you what your project was. Perhaps you didn't even notice."

"I noticed," she said, smiling as though she wouldn't hold it against me forever.

I compensated by giving her exhibit the attention it deserved. As background to the turning planets, she had a huge poster of the sky with several areas circled. The one around the Big Dipper told me to "See Poster A," which was titled, "The Big Dipper is in the constellation Ursa Major."

"Oh," I said, having trouble making conversation while I recovered from my embarrassment. Besides, I didn't want to talk. I only wanted to stare at her. She had on an orange blouse, which was bright and colorful and attracted attention. "A constellation within a constellation."

"No. Most people think the Big Dipper is a constellation but it's really only a part of the constellation Ursa Major. The Big Bear. See?" She used a pointer and extended a graceful arm and introduced me to the Big Bear.

"Hey! The peacock feather."

"Yes, doesn't it make a great pointer?" She brushed it across my nose, and her smile was more dazzling than any star.

"I'm sorry about what happened last night at Adam's," she said.

"Yeah, well . . ." She was a marvelous distraction from last night and I didn't know what to say, so I involved myself in her exhibit again.

"Now learn a couple of stars," she said, hypnotizing me with the peacock feather. "Follow the arc of the handle to Arcturus, then go in a spike to Spica."

"Hey, neat. That's easy enough." I thought my grin was going to pop right off my face.

"This middle star on the handle of the Dipper is really two stars, called a double star."

"How did you find out about it?" I asked, realizing at once that my question was totally out of context.

She astonished me by knowing exactly what I meant. "It was on the news this morning."

This was easy, this talking to a girl, this particular girl. Why had I tortured myself thinking it was hard?

"I think it's terrible," she said. "I don't know why people can't just appreciate one another instead of being so hateful."

She must have wondered at my little laugh, but I was thinking she would fit right in with my family. The bell rang and made me jump, surprised to realize we were in a large, noisy hubbubing room and not out there quietly in the stars at all.

"Got to go," I said abruptly, and I got. I was a little wobbly from the joy of Annajoy and from the fact that I wasn't set up. If the equipment was there it would only take a minute. If it wasn't, well, I had a problem.

Brod was already there and that was a shock, too. In my mind I'd left him there on the sidewalk as though he would remain there forever. Before Annajoy I had been a little prepared for seeing Brod. Now I felt stripped of all my defenses.

"Why is your face all red?" he asked me at once.

For some reason I knew he meant Annajoy, but I forced my mind to shift to last night and said, "You ought to know." Certainly having a cross burned in front of your nose was reason enough for a red face.

"What ought I to know? I saw you talking to Annajoy."
He sounded angry, as if I had no right to be talking to her.

I moved to slip my disk into the disk drive slot and it
bumped his disk, which was already in. I felt stupid for reveal-
ing my distraction, for of course he had everything set up,
with our menu on the screen. In lieu of looking at Brod, I
looked at the screen.

Fun with Computers
Press the corresponding number to see what you want.

1. Learn More About Computers
2. Play Kingdom of Leaves
3. Play Galactic Warriors
4. Play How to Destroy the Enemy

At that moment I knew what to do with an enemy. I was
going to quit being a pacifist and trounce him. Or try.

"I was just deleting it," he said, and he keyed into the file,
highlighted "How to Destroy the Enemy," and we nearly
fought over the delete key.

"What do you think you're doing?"

He deleted it, which deleted it from the disk. I quit the
program, popped out his disk, and inserted mine.

"It's gone," he said. "I deleted it."

"I don't trust you." I still hadn't even looked at him.

"I put it in the other day because I was mad about you and
Annajoy."

Ah, he knew.

"I changed my mind this morning but didn't have time to
take it out after I heard the news."

So he wasn't ignorant about what had happened last night.

My mouth was all screwed around in anger and my head snapped to look at him. His face was a mess, all banged up, bright with bruises.

"Brod. Your face. How did *your* face get so red?"

"I fell out of Lover's Oak this morning." He laughed. Typical Broderick. He could get banged up and act like it was funny.

My first thought was what might have happened to the poster. It looked fine. "How come the poster didn't get bashed?"

"I tossed it away as I went down. Quick thinking, eh?"

The menu came up on the screen without the Enemy game. But I thought he'd removed it just because I had come. I didn't trust him not to copy it back in.

"Brod, your disk." I held out my hand, and to my surprise, looking miserable but with no protest, he placed it in my palm. "Do you have a copy?" I knew he did. It was a computer rule to always make a backup copy because sometimes a disk went kaflooey.

"At home. But I'll delete it."

"Brod, where did you get that horrible game?"

"Germany."

"I don't mean Germany. You didn't go to Germany to get it. I mean where did *you* get it?"

He shrugged and we moved aside for students who were coming up to explore the computer.

"Your father? Did you get this from your father?"

A girl at the computer had pressed "2" and Kingdom of Leaves came up on the screen.

"I see you renamed your game," Brod said. "It's great how

you made the tree drop the leaves, then form a castle as they pile up toward the top of the screen." So he had looked at my program again, and I had not looked at his. I hoped he hadn't done anything stupid, like—I gasped at the thought—put the Enemy game in place of his game so it wouldn't show on the menu.

"Excuse me just a minute," I said to the girl at the computer. I almost nudged her aside as I leaned over to the keyboard and quit my leaf game and clicked into Galactic Warriors.

"Yeahhh!" said the boys in the group when spaceships showed up on the screen, and "Awww" when I clicked it off and returned to the leaf game. Saying, "Sorry, I had to check something," I turned the keyboard back over to the girl.

I pocketed Brod's disk, said I was going to walk around, and I walked.

"You're not going to stay and watch people play our games?" he asked to my back.

Obviously, I wasn't. I kept walking. First I swung by Annajoy's exhibit again, but she wasn't there. I kept my eye sharp for her black hair and orange blouse, but the place was crowded and buzzing and there seemed to be a sea of orange shirts and blouses.

I sought out Adam. I was ready to talk about last night and hoped he was, too, but no. His exhibit was mobbed and he was basking in the glory. "First place" flicked through my head. Adam would get it, not me and Brod. That was okay. Maybe it was even better, under the circumstances.

I ran into Molo at his exhibit, drops of water from creek, pond, river, and ocean to look at under a microscope. It was always fascinating to see what monsters lurked in a drop of water, but it wasn't very creative. Three slides, each under a microscope, with labels saying where the water came from and identifying some of the creatures in the water. How long could that have taken?

"Science gives me grief," he said. "I'd rather have a music fair."

"That would give *me* grief," I said.

"Nah, man. Your parents are musicians like mine are."

"Yeah, but I didn't inherit the talent." We moved aside for kids to look through the microscopes.

"How's your exhibit going?" he asked.

I glanced down an aisle toward our exhibit, saying good-bye to any hopes for first place, and I could have kicked myself. There was Annajoy at our exhibit talking to Brod and here I was walking around looking for her and the bell rang and I had to get to homeroom to collect my books and head to second period.

# Chapter Twelve

**A**s soon as we were settled in Ms. Johnson's room for history, she announced that Mr. Hamlin's homeroom class would be joining us for a few minutes. We did this occasionally, usually when there was something they wanted us to talk about, such as when two of our schoolmates were killed in an accident last year. Who decided which classes to combine? We all knew what was going to be discussed, and Brod would be with the other group. I shimmied over and beckoned for Adam to come sit with me.

"What do you think?" I whispered to him.

"It's okay with me."

I wasn't sure it was all right with me, but I didn't see that anyone was asking me.

The other class came in, found seats, and everyone settled down without having to be told. The quiet mood was a startling change after the hubbub in the cafeteria.

Ms. Johnson started off by saying that the school board, the superintendent, faculty, parents, and others who cared about us thought we should all have a chance to talk about "the incident that took place in our community last night."

"I assume," she said, "that everyone knows about this event. Is there anyone here who doesn't?"

No one. Unless they were out of town or had their head in a sack, they had to know. The school yard and halls had been filled with it.

"Does anyone want to say how they feel about it?"

"I think it's terrible. And scary," said a girl from Mr. Hamlin's class.

This was followed by a series of "Me too's."

"I think it's terrible that this late in history people haven't yet learned how to quit warring and hating and to appreciate one another without reference to race . . ."

Several people joined, like a chorus, ". . . creed, color, religious beliefs, or sexual orientation."

Then Jeff Jarvis stunned everyone by saying, "I thought it was pretty exciting." There was a collective gasp by those of us who disagreed and perhaps by those who agreed but didn't want to say so.

"I hate hate," someone else offered.

"But that's hate, too," said Annajoy, which triggered a hundred discussions inside me.

"You hate the sin but not the sinner," Walt Lundblad said.

My mind was turning, turning on how you accomplished such a trick. How could I respect opinions when some of them were like Brod's? I wondered how Brod felt about sitting in the midst of such a discussion. I had no doubt Mr. Shaw was involved and I wondered if there were other kids who knew their fathers were involved.

"I don't like to think we have people like that in Hanover."

"There are people like that everywhere."

"What about these people who come to our country and take our jobs and refuse to learn our language and act strange?" Jeff again.

"I didn't come to this country," Molo said. "I was born here, man. I speak the same language you do. And my ancestors who came didn't come because they won a vacation cruise to America."

"And what do you think is strange about me?" Adam asked. "Is it my black hair? My dark eyes? My dark skin? Or just that I'm fluent in Spanish and you're not?"

"I wasn't talking about you," Jeff said.

"The cross was burned in his yard, you jerk, so who are you talking about?"

"That was your house?" Jeff had heard the news but not all of the news. A name like Festivo couldn't belong to anyone else but Adam and his family. "I didn't know that. Why did they burn it at your house? And no, I don't think you're strange."

"We're all strange, man," someone said.

"Especially you."

"I like meeting different people. And just because someone's strange doesn't give anyone the right to talk hateful about them."

"We have the right to say whatever we want to about it," Jeff said. "The Supreme Court says so."

"It's a good question Adam asks," Mr. Hamlin said. "What makes someone 'strange,' as you call it? We don't want to horrify you with stories and pictures of the terrible things people have done to one another in this world, but I know you look at the newspaper and listen to the news if for no other reason than your current events homework." Some of us laughed and looked at Ms. Johnson. She was the one who required the current events. She was always telling us we should know our history but that "history is not just the past. History is now."

"World War II was before my time, too," she said, "but you need to study a bit about what happened to the Jews at that time. There have been horror stories all through history, the more recent being 'ethnic cleansing' in the former Yugoslavia. Imagine being taken from your home and family for nothing you have done but just because you are of a certain religion. Imagine being gassed to death in enormous ovens. Imagine someone stealing your rings or even taking the gold out of your teeth when you're lying in a trench for mass burial." She shivered just talking about it. "If you think of where our families came from originally, we are a country of strangers."

We had just been calling out responses but Renee Squirrel held up her hand. "As far as I know," she said, "my people were always from here." We nodded assent. She was half Cherokee.

"What is it that makes us feel strange with one another?" asked Ms. Johnson.

"And why does this make us dislike one another?" added Mr. Hamlin. They must have had a meeting to plan this out.

"I think we're afraid." That was Annajoy again and I was proud of her for speaking up. Proud of Jeff, too, in a way. At least he was saying what he thought and not being quiet about it, like I was. I have lots of thoughts, feelings, and opinions about things but I guess I usually kept them to myself.

"I am not afraid of anything," Jeff said.

Yeah, I thought. It could be Brod talking.

"Then you must be stupid. Everybody with a brain has the sense to be afraid of some things."

"You just told us what you were afraid of," Annajoy said. "You're afraid that they'll get all the jobs. You're afraid because you can't understand their language, so you don't know what they're saying about things."

"Yeah." Randy spoke up. "Once when I was little and we were waiting to buy ice cream, the people next to us were talking another language and I didn't even know there *was* another language. I'd never had the experience of hearing people talk without me knowing what they were saying. I don't understand it to this day, but it frightened me so much that I had a fit and we had to leave without ice cream."

"That makes *you* afraid, not me." Jeff again.

"He just means, bubblehead, that sometimes we are afraid of things we don't understand."

People started popping off all kinds of things. "If you're Korean." "If you're Asian anything." "If you're poor." "If you're rich." "If you're a girl." "If you're skinny." "If you have red hair," which was interrupted with, "Hey, Bri, we love your red hair."

"If you're fat." This stopped the motion of the brainstorming. Harry Hugely was teased double because of his size and his name. He made jokes about himself and was so hilarious he made us laugh and we never thought he minded.

I felt the silence hanging heavy on Harry, so I said one that was on my mind. "If you're old. My grandmother has Alzheimer's, and talk about strange . . ." Some of them laughed and I hadn't meant to make a joke of it. "Sometimes she behaves strangely and people stare at her and at us, like we should keep her home and not take her out anywhere."

"If you're tall." Molo sat taller to emphasize it. "Listen, just because I'm black and tall, people think I'm older than twelve. And I can be walking down the street and people are all suspicious like I'm going to steal their stuff. Man, I don't want their stuff. I just want to get home for supper."

"Well, students," Ms. Johnson said. "You've opened some ideas on an interesting and important subject. I think we have all these varieties of people in our school. Even old, though I'm not there yet."

"I want those who spoke up to write a paper about whatever you mentioned," Mr. Hamlin said.

There was no disagreement whatsoever in the groan that filled the room. "Why do teachers have to turn everything into an assignment?" Adam whispered to me. "I'm glad I kept my mouth shut."

But Mr. Hamlin was going on. "And the rest of you, just pick one of the things that were mentioned, or some prejudice you yourself have felt, or observed, or heard about. If anyone has any problem with what to write about, you can consult either me or Ms. Johnson and we will help you out."

"We all need to know what and why and how we think and feel about these things," Ms. Johnson said. "We need to think about how we are going to run our own lives and develop our own spirits."

"How long does it have to be?"

"When do we have to turn it in?"

"Does it have to be in ink?"

"Another option is to write about possible solutions," Mr. Hamlin said. "We need you students with your bright young minds to come up with some solutions that we adults haven't yet been able to come up with."

The announcement of the science fair winners came as we chomped on our lunches at our desks. Adam had won first place. The whole room burst into whoops of congratulations. I thought they'd kill him pounding on his back. He did have the best exhibit, of course, but because of what had happened last night, this seemed especially fitting. I was surprised to have a twinge at only getting an honorable mention, because I thought I didn't care anymore.

After school, Rosie came to help Adam gather up all his stuff, but all I had to do was pocket my disk and go, so I didn't walk him to the bus. Brod was getting his disk and the poster and he followed me through the cafeteria and out of the building as though he was walking me to the bus. He had as much right to walk this way as I did, but we didn't speak. I could have gone back and waited for Rosie and Adam, but they would be a while and I never thought Brod was *really* following me, just coming along at the same time.

At the gate I turned left toward George Street instead of crossing and going down Albany as usual. Nothing was "usual" anymore, not Nanna, not Brod, not even the way I walked to and from school.

Brod stuck with me. By the time we turned onto George Street we still hadn't spoken and the crowd was thinning.

"Well, does his winning first at the science fair give you another reason to hate Adam?" I asked.

"I don't hate Adam."

"You could have fooled me."

"What did you tell your father?" His voice was a challenge, as though I better not have said anything.

"About what?" I asked, returning the challenge.

"The computer game."

I didn't have to ask if he meant Kingdom of Leaves or Galactic Warriors.

"Nothing until last night."

"Last night?"

In two seconds Brod's face changed expressions so many times it was as though it had fallen apart and put itself back together again. Looking around, then whispering in case any-one was close enough to hear, he said, "I hated that. I didn't know they were going to do that. I didn't think they'd do that to friends. I didn't know anything about it until I was listening to the news this morning, but I knew Dad had been out last night. I . . . I . . . got so mad I . . ."

"You mean you've known about this?" There was no more challenge in his voice, but there was one in mine, though I whispered, too. On Molo's street I didn't want to be heard even talking about this. "You've known about this, that your father is in the Klan?"

"Sure. It's not a secret in the families. We even have family get-togethers. Like picnics."

"Picnics?" I shivered. "Was that you picnicking across the marsh from Adam's yesterday evening?"

He opened his mouth, then closed it.

Did they have a happy meal before they went to burn crosses? I turned to look at his familiar face, that face I'd known for so long, but the face wasn't familiar. It was red, purple, and green with bruises, and something bumped inside me. I had looked at him so little during the day I had forgotten about his face, but I knew with a certainty that he had not fallen out of Lover's Oak.

"Broderick, did your father do that to you?"

For a minute he didn't answer and we kept pace with one another.

"He wanted me to stay home from school."

My eyebrows moved together and down. "He hit you for that?"

"No. Look, he's my father. I can't explain it to you." And he immediately began to explain. "He hates certain people. I can't help it. It's not my fault. And when Adam showed us the picture of the Klan, I guess it made me afraid and frustrated, then angry at the same people my father stays angry with."

Whoosh. I remembered that it was the day Adam showed us that picture that Brod jumped Molo and spewed venom about him and Adam.

"I wanted to be angry at everybody. Then later when you stopped working with me on the project and I found out you were working with Annajoy, well, I wanted to get even, and I knew just how to do it. Then this morning when I found out *where* they'd burned the cross, I changed my mind and didn't want to use the Enemy game, but things got rather busy and I didn't have time to delete it from the disk before I left for school."

Whoosh, whoosh, whoosh. My innards were moving around in me like a tidal wave. I was surprised to see we'd turned the corner toward my house. Even this was backward. All these years we had come to his house first. I didn't want him to go home. I didn't want him to have to face a father like that. I remembered speaking up to Mr. Shaw when I was five years old and I was ready to do it again. I knew the fear of violence more strongly than I did before last night because I knew if I spoke up to Brod's father, he wouldn't do a thing to me. He'd do it to Brod. I wanted things to be the same as always, but "always" was gone forever.

"Come in with me?"

"You mean it?"

I curled my arm around his neck and gave him a squeeze. "Sure."

We heard Mom and Nanna in the kitchen and Brod whispered again. "Do they know?"

Mom did, but who knew what Nanna knew? By the time I shrugged, we were there.

"Well, hello, boys," Mom said, masking her surprise so it was hardly noticeable. I remembered Rosie telling Adam, that first day with Nanna, to just pretend she hadn't shown us her room a zillion times. So I pretended Brod being here with me was perfectly normal, just as I'd pretended "normal" after the Molo incident. I opened the refridge and handed Brod juice and fruit. Just two boys getting a snack after school. As we'd done a hundred times.

Dad strolled in from the studio and Brod got all nervous,

not looking at Dad and rocking from one foot to the other. Then he sat at the kitchen table and lowered his head onto one arm and covered it with the other.

"Now what? I guess the boys have been fussing again." Nanna took a seat at the table.

Dad, Mom, and I remained standing.

"Mother," Dad said, "I think I need to talk with the boys privately, so if you two will excuse us we'll adjourn to the porch. Sorry, Claudi."

"It's quite all right, sweetheart."

"Okay, Brod?" Dad asked as Brod vacated the table.

Mom took a seat. "Mother Vee, let's sit here and have some tea."

We followed Dad to the porch, where he sat on the swing. Broderick sat in the rocker and gripped the fat wooden arms as if to hang on for dear life. Somehow I had a sense of the balance, here, as if to almost make myself disappear. I unfolded one of the low lawn chairs and sat several feet away from Brod and almost behind him.

I saw Dad see Brod's face, part his lips to speak, change his mind and close them.

"Mr. Viravek, I'm sorry and embarrassed about last night. I didn't know they were going to do that."

I could barely hear him because he was speaking to his chest. Dad nodded, and then Nanna walked onto the porch. She eyed the other low lawn chair and the spot by Dad on the swing and opted for the swing. Dad, Brod, and I didn't move, we barely even breathed.

"Oh, don't let me bother you," Nanna said. "Just go right ahead. I've just come to look at my birds."

Brod gave Dad a pleading look.

"It's nothing you want to hear, Nanna," I said.

"Oh, I'm eighty years old. What does it matter? I guess I've heard everything by now."

I wondered what she remembered about last night. Once I would have thought that surely anyone would remember fiery torches and men in white robes. But a few minutes after she'd cut onions and prepared the squash casserole she had asked who made it.

Standing quietly at the door, Mom exchanged glances with Dad and unfolded the low lawn chair, sat by Brod, and put a hand on his arm. I was uncomfortable with this becoming a convention. I couldn't imagine us having to do all the repeats Nanna would require.

"It's some stuff about trouble and hatefulness, Nanna. You don't want to hear it." I sort of made a face to make her want to leave the porch.

"Hate? Oh, I know about hate," she said. "That's why I came to this country, to get away from hate. During World War II we lived through all the atrocities from the Germans. My boys and I lived through them, that is. My husband was killed during them, during the war. It wasn't just war, soldiers killing soldiers or civilians being caught in the cross fire, but there was killing of certain other people just because of their name or their religion or their language or because they had the wrong color eyes."

She could be taking part in our discussion at school. I glanced at Broderick, wondering what he thought about what had been said in class and how he felt about it, being closely connected with one of the people responsible. "After the war was finally over and the Germans were defeated and we could at last have peace, we didn't have peace. In anger from having suffered so many horrors, my very own dear Czechoslovakian people were hungry to have revenge, retaliation, retribution. They began to commit the same atrocities against the Germans or anyone they thought might be German or anyone who might have been friendly with a German. Instead of being relieved that it was finally over, as I was, they wanted to do to someone else the same things that had been done to us. No matter who is doing it, an atrocity is still an atrocity. I don't understand it. I didn't want to kill someone just because my beloved Jovan, father of my little boys, had been killed. I just wanted the violence to stop. It broke my heart."

I knew these stories but hadn't paid enough attention. They'd just drifted into some sideways place in me, out of sight, nearly out of memory. That was the most I'd heard Nanna say since she came to our house. Dad had his hand on her knee. Of course I knew the stories, I reminded myself. I just had never connected them with anything to do with life. Until now.

"It broke my heart," Nanna repeated once, quietly. I guess it had already run around inside her as much as she could stand. Nanna had come here years ago, in exile. And now it struck me like a kick. In her new, strange version of reality, where she was lost to us and we were lost to her and she was even lost to herself, Nanna was in exile again.

# *Afterword*

I looked at Brod and thought of the atrocity of hate, the atrocity of burning a cross. The atrocity of having your father hit you. The atrocity of losing a friend.

A car pulled into the driveway and here came Adam and Rosie to lighten our mood. There was a round of congratulations for Adam, and Nanna joined in, too, "Though I don't know what I'm congratulating you for."

"He won first place at the science fair," Broderick said. If he was disappointed, he didn't show it.

"Oh, the science fair," Nanna said. "What did you do at the science fair?"

Adam told her about his project, and no sooner had he finished than she repeated her question. I thought invitations to see her room would be next.

This time he only said, "I did a project on the environment," and kept on talking. Rosie had brought his camera with Patrick's attachments to school and he thought he got some great pictures. "On the way home we're going to stop

*158*

and see if I can get some good shots of the hawk. Want to come?"

Broderick lit up at the idea and I saw the adults raise eyebrows at one another. Brod couldn't have missed it.

Very quietly Dad said, "Not today, Broderick. Maybe another time."

And in perfect timing, a bellow roared out over the neighborhood.

"Bro-o-o-od."

Brod slumped, then hunched a shoulder and stood up. "Well, I guess I have to go, anyway."

"Broderick, will you be all right?" I asked.

"Oh, yeah." He hunched again.

I followed him down the stairs. "If you need any help, you come here, okay?"

He didn't say if he would or wouldn't, but by the time he reached the street his shoulders were back and he made long strides for home.

"Any new news?" Rosie was asking when I returned to the porch.

"The police have not yet identified any of the perpetrators," Dad said.

All of them were watching Brod. I understood Brod not telling me more, not wanting them to know, not knowing they did, anyway. How in the world did you point a finger at your own father?

"Come on, go with us," Rosie said. "We'll bring you back."

"I'd like to go, too," Nanna said, standing up and ready.

"Sure. You can all come. Mom, Dad, there's room for everyone." She drove a wide pickup with a backseat.

"No, you all just go on. We'll stay here." Dad slid an arm around Mom's waist. I knew what they were thinking. Ahhh, a few minutes without Nanna. "Grab the binoculars."

I did.

As we drove down off the River Bridge we spotted the hawk on top of a pole. Rosie pulled over and stopped before we were too close. Nanna and I had learned long ago that it had a specific distance it would let you come before it flew. She had once called that its comfort zone.

Adam lifted his equipment from the car and Nanna started walking toward the hawk. The ground was uneven and she was tottering. Afraid she would fall, I called out, "Nanna, be careful, you might fall," and I started toward her.

"Oh, I'm eighty years old," she said. Then waving her arms and shouting, "Shoo, shoo, shoo," to the hawk, she forgot to finish her remark. "We want to see you fly."

The hawk spread wings, dropped from the top of the pole, banked and gave us a view of his red shoulders. As I raised the binoculars and heard the *click-click-click* of Adam's camera, the hawk soared into forever.